HOMECOMING

Lizzie is the sixth and youngest daughter of the late Sir Beverley, the patriarch who gambled away their beloved estate, Mannerling. Each of Lizzie's sisters had been entrusted by their ambitious mother to lure the various owners of their former home. Instead, each one married for love. Now it's Lizzie's turn to save Mannerling. Yet the new owner, the Duke of Severnshire, is far too arrogant for Lizzie's heart. And while the duke has no intentions toward Lizzie, her curt dismissal is perplexing — for no woman has ever refused him! Soon thoughts turn away from a suitable marriage — to the wonders of falling in love!

M. C. BEATON

HOMECOMING

Complete and Unabridged

PUBLISHER SELECTION
Leicester

First published in Great Britain in 2014 by
Canvas
an imprint of Constable & Robinson Ltd
London

First Ulverscroft Edition
published 2018
by arrangement with
Little, Brown Book Group
An Hachette UK Company
London

A catalogue record for this book is available
from the British Library.

ISBN 978–1–4448–3858–9

Published by
F. A. Thorpe (Publishing)
Anstey, Leicestershire

Set by Words & Graphics Ltd.
Anstey, Leicestershire
Printed and bound in Great Britain by
T. J. International Ltd., Padstow, Cornwall

This book is printed on acid-free paper

*This series is dedicated to
Rosemary Barradell with love*

ONE

What's the good of a home if you are never in it?
  GEORGE AND WEEDON GROSSMITH

Brookfield House, home of the Beverleys, was an unassuming place, nothing like their previous grand property, Mannerling. It was a square country building of grey stone with neat sash windows and a plain front door without pediment or portico.

It was hardly the setting for the dramatic scene that was taking place in front of it.

The great Duke of Severnshire stood there, tall, haughty and every inch the aristocrat, from his tall beaver hat and proud nose to his glossy Hessian boots.

Standing in front of him was the Beverleys' governess, elderly but fashionably dressed and with clever sparkling eyes in a wrinkled face and, under a modish cap, brown hair which did not show a trace of grey. The youngest of the Beverley sisters, Lizzie, stood defiantly beside her governess, her green eyes blazing, for this haughty duke had found her visiting Mannerling, her old home, told her it was now his property, and had told her to get off it.

Lady Beverley was all amazement, her pale eyes goggling. For the Duke of Severnshire, whom she had often longed to meet, was actually here on

1

her doorstep and claiming that the governess, Miss Trumble, was his aunt!

'I repeat my question, Aunt Letitia,' said the duke frostily: 'What are you doing here?'

'I wish to speak to my nephew in private, Lady Beverley,' said Miss Trumble quietly.

'Of course. By all means,' said Lady Beverley, shaken to the core. 'Pray use the parlour, Miss Trumble.'

Miss Trumble and the tall duke went into the house and into the parlour, and the duke firmly closed the door behind them.

'Come away, Mama,' hissed Lizzie as Lady Beverley pressed an ear against the door panels.

At that moment, the duke jerked open the door again. Lady Beverley jumped back. 'Oh, Your Grace,' she cried. 'I was just about to enter and ask if you desired any refreshment.'

'No!' he said, and slammed the door in her face.

'Insufferable,' said Lizzie, taking her mother's arm and guiding her into the drawing-room across the hall.

'I do not understand,' wailed Lady Beverley. 'Our Miss Trumble aunt to the duke? There must be some mistake.'

'I do not think so,' said Lizzie. 'There was always a mystery about our Miss Trumble. You always said her gowns were too fine for a governess. And if she had to escort us to a function in London, she always disguised herself in a dreadful wig.'

Lady Beverley sat down. 'Perhaps he might buy Mannerling.'

Time and again Lady Beverley had been

thwarted in her schemes of regaining her old home: plots that had been built around one of her six daughters marrying one of the owners. But owners had come and gone and Lizzie's five elder sisters had all married other men, much to Lady Beverley's chagrin. With the exception of Lizzie, damned with a fey appearance and unfashionable red hair, the Beverley sisters were all famous for their beauty.

'The duke has already bought Mannerling,' said Lizzie.

'But he has a great palace of his own,' exclaimed Lady Beverley. 'What can he want with Mannerling?'

'I neither know nor care,' said Lizzie.

Lady Beverley focused on her youngest daughter. 'Tish, what is to be done with you, Lizzie? You look like a schoolgirl. Severnshire is unmarried still, I believe. If only one of your sisters were still unwed! What hope is there with the runt of the litter?'

This last was said in a low voice, not really meant for Lizzie's ears, but Lizzie heard it and flushed miserably.

'How did you know he had bought Mannerling?' demanded Lady Beverley.

'I heard it from Barry.' Barry was the odd man. Lizzie decided she must warn him that he was supposed to have told her, for she did not want her mother to know that she had gone for a look round her old home and had been told to leave by the duke.

'Imagine Miss Trumble being his aunt. Dear me, she cannot possibly stay with us now. I wonder what her real name is? Lady Something, and she will exceed me in rank! I wonder what they are talking about? I wonder why she decided to become a mere governess? Scandal. It must have been because of some dreadful scandal. I wish I could hear what they are talking about.'

The duke was pacing up and down the small parlour. 'Do sit down, Gervase, and stop towering over me,' begged Miss Trumble.

He sat down in an armchair and stretched out his long legs. 'Why Trumble, of all stupid names?' he demanded.

'It was the name of my old nurse. I was very fond of her.'

'You had no need to go out and find employ.'

'Can you not understand that I was bored, Gervase? A spinster lady, a tiresome relation, not really wanted anywhere. I have been needed here, am still needed here.'

'You cannot possibly stay here now you have been discovered!'

'But only by you. A few of my old friends, Lady Evans, for example, who lives on the other side of Hedgefield, know of my true identity, and they will not speak of it, so why should you?'

'Such a position with such a family!'

'What is up with them?!'

'I have been long enough in the neighbourhood to pick up the gossip. Sir William Beverley lost everything at the card tables and so had to sell up, and ever since then the Beverleys have done nothing but plot and scheme to find ways of getting Mannerling back.'

'The five elder Beverleys have all married well, and to gentlemen they love. There is only little Lizzie left and I intend to stay in my post until she is wed.'

'That odd, rude little girl! I found her wandering about Mannerling as if she owned the place and sent her to the right about.'

'Oh dear.'

'Besides, it harms my dignity to have you here.'

'Oh, Gervase, that wretched family pride. I once shared it and it destroyed my chance at happiness.'

He raised his thin eyebrows in query.

'I was courted by an army captain. This is very old family history. I was very much attracted to him. But I was persuaded by my father that he was an adventurer, only interested in my money. I was taught to rate my looks very low, rather like poor Lizzie, and so I let him go. He was killed in battle. How I mourned! But' – she gave a little smile – 'that is surely of no interest to you. I became interested in learning and then, as the years passed, I had a hunger to pass that learning on. I am persuaded that had the Beverley girls not had a good education and well-trained minds, then they would have succumbed to disastrous marriages.'

'But you must remember you are Lady Letitia Revine, my late father's sister, and your situation here is a scandal and a disgrace.'

'No worthwhile work is a scandal or a disgrace. I promised Lizzie I would stay until she was wed, and so I shall. Until that time I am Miss Trumble, governess.'

'That little redhead will not take. Too farouche.'

'Lizzie has character and charm. You have not seen her at her best.'

'How old is she? Sixteen?'

'Nineteen now and of an age to be wed.'

'That is Lady Beverley's concern, not yours.'

'I have made it mine, Gervase. I suggest you go away and forget you have found me. Why did you buy Mannerling? You have no need of the place.'

'It is a fine place and I always increase my holdings and property when I can. I thought it might be a fitting property for my son when he comes of age.'

Miss Trumble blinked. 'I did not even know you were married. I heard nothing about it.'

'I am not married ... yet, but I plan to change that situation as soon as possible.'

'You have found someone?'

'No, but I shall. It is difficult to find someone suitable to my rank.'

'Oh, Gervase, I despair of you!'

'To my rank,' he repeated firmly. 'Mannerling is a pretty setting. I shall invite some suitable prospects from time to time. I desire a son.'

'There are a great number of so-called ordinary people who are well worth knowing, Gervase, and by armouring yourself in rank, you are cutting yourself off from them.'

'I am become expert at cutting myself off from adventuresses, toadies, mushrooms and counter jumpers,' he said coldly. 'Do you really mean you wish me to help you prolong this masquerade?'

'I do not need your help. Simply do not talk about it and I will persuade Lady Beverley to do the same.'

'I never knew a woman yet who could keep a secret.'

'You are looking at one. And be assured that neither Lizzie nor Lady Beverley will speak of it.'

His odd silvery eyes under hooded lids looked at her cynically. 'But Lady Beverley will no doubt see it as a means to push that dreadful little daughter of hers in my direction.'

'I think Lizzie has taken you in dislike. I will not be encouraging any matchmaking. I am very fond of Lizzie. She is too good for you, and too young. How old are you now? Thirty-four?'

The duke nodded.

'Nearly twice her age. But, Gervase, as your neighbours, Lady Beverley and Lizzie should be invited to dinner or to one of your parties.'

'I do not see why I should.'

'Because if you do not, I will make it known I am your aunt.'

'You are blackmailing me, Aunt Letitia!'

'Yes, I suppose I am. Shall we join the ladies? And do address me as Miss Trumble. I am accustomed to the name and by virtue of its long use, it has become my own.'

He wondered briefly if madness ran in his family, but the eyes surveying him were bright, intelligent and mocking. His aunt, he realized ruefully, was managing to make him feel like a pompous fool.

'Very well,' he said with a sudden charming smile.

'I shall summon them.' Miss Trumble rose to her feet.

'Ring the bell for a servant.'

'You forget, I am a servant.'

It was as well for Lizzie that her mother was non-plussed. Her own governess outranking her!

Lady Beverley entered the parlour very sub-dued, and curtsied low to the duke. Then she turned to Miss Trumble.

'I do not know how to address you.'

'I shall be remaining in your employ, my lady,' said Miss Trumble. 'And Miss Trumble is my name.'

'But His Grace said–'

'We will forget what my nephew said. I pro-mised Lizzie I would remain until she was wed.'

'Oh, my best of governesses,' said Lizzie, her eyes shining. 'I thought you would leave me.'

'Make your curtsy to His Grace, Lizzie, and be seated.'

Lizzie gave a bob of a curtsy and sat down.

Lady Beverley ordered tea. Her mind was begin-ning to race. Here was the Duke of Severnshire in her parlour, the *unwed* Duke of Severnshire, and his aunt was Lizzie's governess. She glanced impatiently at Lizzie. The child ought to have put her hair up.

But still trying to assimilate the fact that Miss Trumble was an aristocrat kept Lady Beverley quiet and correct where normally she would have bored the duke to flinders with apocryphal tales of the greatness of the Beverley family and she would have made her great ambition to possess Mannerling all too clear.

Out of courtesy to Miss Trumble, Lizzie was

polite and respectful to the duke, although privately she considered him cold and haughty. Because he was a duke, most ladies would immediately think him handsome. But she found his great height and cold silvery eyes unnerving. His hair was worn long and confined at his neck with a ribbon. His clothes were impeccable and she wondered why he wore his hair in such an old-fashioned manner when most gentlemen now wore a Brutus crop or the Windswept.

'Why are you looking at me so curiously, Miss Lizzie?' asked the duke suddenly.

'I was wondering why you bought Mannerling when you have no need of the place,' said Lizzie, startled into saying the second thing in her mind, not wanting to ask him about his hair.

'As I have already explained to my aunt, it struck me that the place might do for my son.'

'Your son!' exclaimed Lady Beverley.

'His Grace is a trifle premature,' said Miss Trumble.

He smiled and Lizzie thought that his smile altered his whole appearance, making him look almost approachable.

'I do not understand,' wailed Lady Beverley, over-set by the idea that this duke was already married.

'I plan to become married soon,' said the duke patiently. 'I would like to secure an heir.'

'I hope you find a suitable lady to breed for you,' said Lizzie.

There was a shocked silence.

'The weather has been very fine for the time of year,' said Miss Trumble, after casting a chilly look in Lizzie's direction. The duke, Miss Trumble, and Lady Beverley began to converse about the English weather.

Lizzie wondered whether it might be possible to die from shame. What had prompted her unruly tongue to make such a remark? She could feel herself blushing hot and red, hear a roaring in her ears through which the polite conversation of the others came faintly.

At last, she could bear her shame no longer. She rose and curtsied to the duke. 'Excuse me, Your Grace,' she muttered and fled the room.

Inside, Lady Beverley felt she should apologize for her daughter's rudeness but then, because the duke appeared calm and pleasant, decided hopefully that he had misheard Lizzie or had not heard her at all.

But when he had taken his leave of her, the duke stopped outside his carriage, turned to Miss Trumble and said coldly, 'The bad behaviour of your charge does you no credit at all, Aunt. I am shocked.'

'Lizzie is an independently minded young lady and *you* shocked *her*.'

'Indeed. What on earth did I say?'

'It was your statement that you were looking for someone to bear you a son. Such is the way of the world, we both know that. But to any intelligent and sensitive lady, the idea of being married simply to bear children, no question of love and affection or even respect, must appear repugnant.'

'If you had perhaps not addled your brain with romances at an early age,' said the duke waspishly, 'you might not be a spinster.'

'That remark, my nephew, was worse than any-thing Lizzie could come up with. Had I addled my brain with romances at an early age rather than being wrapped up in pride and consequence, then I might have known some happiness before my captain was killed. Good day to you.'

Miss Trumble turned and went in search of Lizzie.

Lizzie was in the small stable with Barry Wort, the odd man, when she heard Miss Trumble's voice. 'Do not betray me, Barry,' she whispered. 'I am in the suds.'

'Lizzie? Where are you?' Miss Trumble again.

Like conspirators, the odd man and Lizzie waited in silence until they heard Miss Trumble's voice again, but fainter this time and going away towards the house.

'Now, miss,' said Barry comfortably, 'what have you been and done now?'

'Such news, Barry. Our Miss Trumble is actually the Duke of Severnshire's aunt.'

'Never!'

'True, Barry.'

'My, my. I always suspected she was a great lady. I'm fair stunned, miss. How is her ladyship taking it?'

'Mama is a trifle dazed.'

'Miss Lizzie, does that mean Miss Trumble will be leaving us?'

'Oh, no; she said she would stay until I was wed.'

'Doesn't make sense to me. Great duke like that

won't want his auntie working as a governess.'

'He has bought Mannerling.'

'So I heard only an hour ago. Why?'

'He says he wants it for his son. He is not even married. He said he would find a suitable woman to bear him one and I opened my mouth and said I hoped he would find someone to breed for him.'

Barry clicked his tongue in an admonitory way. 'That was not good, miss.'

'And that is why Miss Trumble is looking for me. Oh, and Barry, I lied and said you had told me he had bought Mannerling, so you must back me up.'

'Best go out there and get it over with.'

'I suppose so. Barry, how are we to treat Miss Trumble now? Miss Trumble is gone. We now have the duke's aunt. Will she move to Mannerling, think you? Will he really let her stay here?'

'I do not see how she can possibly stay here,' said Barry sadly. 'Nothing will be the same if she goes.'

'I cannot hide here,' said Lizzie. 'I will be brave. I will go and see her.'

Barry has turned suddenly old, she thought as she left. His round face, usually cheerful, looked wrinkled and careworn and his shoulders stooped.

'Lizzie!' cried Miss Trumble, coming out of the house as she approached. 'I would speak with you.'

Lizzie walked forward and dropped a curtsy and said, 'My lady?'

'I am still Miss Trumble, Lizzie, and until I finish my employ here, you will address me as such.'

Lizzie's face brightened. 'You are really to stay with us?'

'I gave you my promise, did I not? Now, is it necessary for me to give you a jaw-me-dead over your remark to the duke?'

'No, Miss Trumble. I am deeply ashamed. But he humiliated me.'

'Meaning he found you in Mannerling where you had no right to be and told you to go away?'

'Yes, but he was so contemptuous, so haughty and cold.'

'He finds a young trespasser who looks like a schoolgirl and who is wandering about his home without an invitation. What would you do if you found someone in Brookfield House, walking about the rooms and looking at everything without a by your leave?'

Lizzie hung her head. Miss Trumble put a hand under the girl's chin and lifted up her face.

Wide green eyes stared at her. Lizzie's eyes were pure green without any trace of brown and framed with thick black lashes. That red hair of hers, damned as unfashionable, was thick and with a slight curl and shone with health.

'Yes,' said Miss Trumble, half to herself, 'you might do. But come indoors and let me arrange your hair. It is time to try out a new style.'

'I told Barry who you really are,' said Lizzie.

Miss Trumble paused on the threshold. 'Indeed! Then go to your room, Lizzie, and look out curling tongs and pins and I will be with you quite soon.'

Miss Trumble turned and hurried back round the side of the house. Barry was just emerging

13

from the stable. He bowed low when he saw her.

'Well, Barry,' said Miss Trumble, 'are we still friends?'

'You are no longer a servant, my lady.'

'I am until I finish my work here, Barry. And as I have explained to Lizzie, until that time, Lady Letitia Revine does not exist. I am Miss Trumble and still a servant like you.'

'I never really thought of you as a servant. But what made you stoop so low?'

'I considered it a step up from being an unwanted maiden aunt. I enjoy teaching. It gives me a purpose in life. Lizzie must be married before I go.'

'Miss Lizzie told me she had been rude to the duke.'

'Very rude, Barry.' Miss Trumble sighed. 'At least it might do him some good. No one is *ever* rude to Gervase. As a result, he is too wrapped up in his own consequence. He wishes to find a bride and it amuses him to invite prospects to Mannerling. Mannerling is his latest toy.'

'He will have no difficulty, him being a great duke.'

'No, he will not, and that will be very bad for him.'

Barry scratched his head. 'Reckon Miss Lizzie is too young for him.'

'Oh, much too young.'

'And yet her sisters married men older than themselves.'

'True, but Gervase is set in his ways and arrogance. I would see Lizzie with someone nearer her own age. But he is to entertain and I have

14

made sure that Lizzie and Lady Beverley are to be invited. I shall call on him in a few days' time and persuade him to invite some suitable young man.'

'So how is Lady Beverley taking the news of your status?'

'I do not know. I have not yet spoken to her.'

'She will not know how to go on.'

'I think she will forget very quickly who I really am. Otherwise she might have to concern herself with the welfare of her own daughter, and also with the running of the house. Now, I must go to Lizzie.'

'I'm right glad you are still to be with us, miss.'

'Oh, you will not lose me, Barry. Do not tell anyone my real identity.'

Barry stood and watched her as she crossed the lawn. Then he began to whistle cheerfully as he returned to his work.

The Duke of Severnshire's secretary, Mr Peter Bond, stood respectfully to attention beside his master's desk three days later while the duke mused over several names he had written down. Peter was a tall, thin, awkward man who came from a good but impoverished family. He had not been able to believe his luck when he obtained the post as secretary to the duke only a year ago, the previous secretary having left to take holy orders. But sometimes he felt it was like working for a machine. The duke never seemed aware of him as a person.

'There are two here I might begin with,' said the duke. 'Lady Verity and Miss Celia Charter.

15

We will write and invite the young ladies and their parents for a visit. Well, Lady Verity is past the first blush of youth, but the family is good, as is her dowry. Miss Celia Charter is young but that has the advantage that she can be schooled in our ways. As to the others, the Chumleys, and... What is it, Palk?'

His butler had entered. 'A Miss Trumble is called, Your Grace. She is only governess to the Beverleys, so I told her you would not be available.'

To Peter's surprise, the duke said, 'On the contrary, Palk, I am always available when Miss Trumble calls. Show her up. That will be all, Mr Bond.'

Peter bowed and made his way out, but was longing to stay and see what this governess had to say to his master.

'Aunt Letitia,' said the duke, rising. 'Pray be seated. Tea, some wine?'

'Tea, I think,' said Miss Trumble, drawing off her gloves. The duke rang the bell and ordered tea. They talked of general matters until the tea was served and the servants had retired.

'How go your plans to wed?' asked Miss Trumble.

'I have selected two initially to see how they go on. Lady Verity and Miss Celia Charter.'

Miss Trumble searched in the files of her capacious memory. 'Lady Verity is not yet wed, daughter of the Earl and Countess of Hernshire; matches you, Gervase, in pride and arrogance. Well enough in looks, as you probably know.'

'I have never met either lady.'

'You amaze me! Did you not see them at a Season?'

'I do not visit the Season. I have spent many years travelling.'

'Miss Celia Charter made her first come-out this year. She is fair and flighty.'

'From my researches I gather she has a good dowry.'

'And what is that to you, rich as you are?'

'It saves me from the perils of being trapped by a fortune-hunter. I do not want to be married for my money.'

'Really, Gervase! And yet you cold-bloodedly select two ladies because you know they are comfortably endowered!'

'May I remind you, Aunt, you are not *my* governess.'

'And more's the pity. I would have schooled you better.'

'As you schooled Lizzie? I should be sitting in drawing-rooms by this time making impertinent remarks to my betters.'

'Lizzie probably does not see you as her better, but she is suitably contrite. I wish you to invite Lady Beverley and Lizzie tomorrow to take tea.'

'This is ridiculous. Oh, very well.' He rang the bell and asked the footman who answered it to find his secretary. Peter came in and stood humbly to attention.

'Mr Bond, be so good as to send a footman to Brookfield House directly inviting Lady Beverley and Miss Lizzie Beverley to tea on the morrow at four o'clock.'

'Very good, Your Grace.'

Peter bowed low and went out.

'I hope that young man eats enough,' said Miss Trumble sharply. 'And he does not look happy.'

'He does his job well, Aunt, so what is it to me if he is unhappy or not?'

'Are you never moved by ordinary human kindness, Gervase?'

'I pay my servants well and they are housed and fed. Your descent to the common state has made you common, Aunt.'

Miss Trumble raised her brows and studied him.

'I beg your pardon,' he said stiffly.

'It is not only my Lizzie, you see, who has a wayward tongue.'

'Will you accompany the Beverleys?'

'Of course. I am also chaperone to Lizzie.'

'May I point out that such a chit as Lizzie Beverley needs no chaperone with me around?'

She smiled. 'Nonetheless, I shall come. Which brings me to the second reason for my visit. When you invite your guests, could you include a suitable young man of good family for my Lizzie?'

He sighed but rang the bell and summoned his secretary again.

'Mr Bond,' he said, 'be so good when you invite the others to include an invitation to some suitable young man. We are desirous of finding a husband for Miss Lizzie Beverley. Does she have a dowry?'

'She will have a fair one,' said Miss Trumble, privately thinking that she would do all in her power to shake a good one out of the cheese-paring Lady Beverley.

'Then see to it, Mr Bond.'

'Very good, Your Grace.'

'Mr Bond!' Miss Trumble summoned him back as he was about to bow his way out of the room.

'Madam?'

'We wish someone of spirit and intelligence and good humour.'

'Very good, Miss Trumble.'

'You know who I am?'

'I made it my business to find out everyone who resides in the neighbourhood of Mannerling, madam.'

'You are an excellent young man. Do you eat enough?'

Peter blushed and looked towards his master but the duke had crossed to the window and was staring out. 'Yes, madam. His Grace has the best chef in the country.'

'Do not eat too much rich food, Mr Bond,' said Miss Trumble, 'and go for walks in the fresh air.'

'Yes, madam.'

'When is your day off?'

'I get one day off every quarter-day, madam.'

'Tisk. You must find time for yourself.'

He bowed out again.

The duke swung round angrily. 'You forget yourself, Aunt. He is my servant and he will work any hours that I choose.'

'He does not look strong,' she said mildly. She drew on her gloves and picked up her reticule. 'Until tomorrow, Gervase.'

Lady Beverley accepted the invitation to tea as her due. She had decided that Miss Trumble

19

must have committed some grave scandal to have reduced her to her present lowly position and therefore there was no need to treat her any differently.

To Miss Trumble's relief, Lizzie showed no joy at the prospect of a visit to Mannerling. The governess was always frightened that the old Beverley obsession with getting Mannerling back would rise again in Lizzie.

But Miss Trumble was irritated, when they climbed into the small carriage driven by Barry, that Lady Beverley did not even seem to notice her daughter's new modish appearance. The day was sunny and warm. Great clouds like galleons under full sail moved in stately procession across a blue sky. Lizzie's red hair was dressed in one of the new Roman fashions and curled and pomaded so that it almost seemed to shine with purple lights. She was wearing a light leaf-green muslin gown with a broad green silk sash. A little straw hat was perched at a jaunty angle on her curls.

Lizzie felt strange and not quite like herself. Clothes were a comfort, she thought. In such a modish gown and with her smart new hairstyle, she was sure she would behave like a lady. 'When in doubt, only speak when spoken to,' Miss Trumble had warned her.

So Lizzie was determined to behave. There would only be herself, Lady Beverley, Miss Trumble, and the duke. Her mother would prose on about the great days of Mannerling when the Beverleys were in residence and Miss Trumble would supply her usual tactful conversation. There would be nothing for her to do but listen and nod from time to time.

But at that moment, the Duke of Severnshire was ringing for his secretary.

When Peter came in, the duke leaned back in his chair and surveyed the young man as if seeing him for the first time. Thin sensitive face, clear grey eyes, fair wispy hair, he was correctly and neatly dressed in black coat and black knee-breeches and square-toed shoes with modest metal buckles.

'Mr Bond,' began the duke, 'as you are aware, the Beverleys are expected, and Miss Trumble.'

'Yes, Your Grace.'

'Miss Lizzie is a tiresome little minx and apt to open her mouth and say the first thing that comes into her head. Very fatiguing. You are to join us and entertain Miss Lizzie. You are to take her away and show her the gardens.'

'Very good, Your Grace.'

'And you may get some of that fresh air Miss Trumble thinks you need so badly.'

'Thank you, Your Grace. I will do my best to entertain Miss Beverley.'

'Ah, so good to be home again!' cried Lady Beverley, sailing into the drawing-room at Mannerling.

'I was under the impression it was *my* home,' said the duke drily.

'You must forgive me,' said Lady Beverley, settling herself on the sofa and looking about her with a complacent air. 'Such happy memories.'

The duke introduced his secretary. He had been a little taken aback by Lizzie's appearance. Quite the little fashion plate, he thought in surprise.

21

'Perhaps Miss Lizzie would care to see the gardens, Mr Bond?'

'Certainly,' said the secretary.

The day had become warm and Lizzie would have liked a cup of tea but she saw the warning flash in Miss Trumble's eyes and rose obediently to her feet.

She and Peter walked down the great staircase. Lizzie looked up at the chandelier.

'Does it still move?' she asked curiously.

'Move, Miss Beverley?'

'A previous owner, a Mr Judd, hanged himself there. Sometimes the chandelier would move and the crystals would tinkle although there was no wind or even a draught.'

'Not that I have heard, Miss Beverley.'

'Strange,' mused Lizzie. 'There is no atmosphere anymore. This house used to feel like a live thing, and sometimes when I entered it seemed to welcome me and from time to time the very walls exuded an air of menace. Now I feel nothing.'

Peter remembered his master's remark that Miss Lizzie came out with whatever happened to be passing through her mind, but he said politely, 'His Grace is so very grand that perhaps his presence has tamed the house.'

'Perhaps,' said Lizzie, as they went out together into the sunlight.

'Do you miss Mannerling very much?'

'I used to,' said Lizzie. 'Yes, very much. But now I think I am quite reconciled to my new home, and it is about time.' Her green eyes flashed with amusement. 'What are you supposed to do with me? Walk me about like a dog?'

Peter suppressed a smile. 'Oh, no, His Grace is all kindness.'

'Do you think I look very fine?'

'Yes, Miss Beverley, very modish.'

Lizzie gave a sigh. 'So let us walk in the gardens. Here is the little lawn at the side where we used to play battledore and shuttlecock.'

'I found bats and shuttlecock in the little cupboard in the Great Hall, and the net.'

'We could play,' said Lizzie eagerly. 'See, the posts for the net are still here.'

'May I point out you are not dressed to play?'

'All I need to do is take off my hat. My kid slippers are perfectly suitable for running across the grass and the modern fashion for loose gowns means I am not constricted in any way.'

'Then we shall play, Miss Beverley.'

They returned to the house, where Peter summoned footmen to put up the net and carry the bats and shuttlecocks round to the side lawn.

Lizzie unpinned her little hat and stripped off her gloves.

'I must warn you, I am a very good player,' she said. 'What about you?'

'Fair, Miss Beverley.'

'I think it would be perfectly in order for you to call me Lizzie when we are not in company since we are destined to be friends.'

Peter looked down at her elfin face and suddenly smiled. 'You may call me Peter, but not in front of my master. He is very strict on protocol.'

'Pooh to your master. Let's play.'

It became all too clear to the duke as Lady

Beverley spoke on that she was still determined to get Mannerling back. 'Such a pity a fine gentleman like yourself is unwed,' she said coyly. 'What you need is a young girl who knows the tenants and the neighbouring aristocracy and gentry.'

'Why a young girl?'

'You will wish to school her in your ways.'

'What a truly dreadful idea,' he said acidly.

'Indeed it is,' put in Miss Trumble maliciously. 'I heard someone else say that just recently.'

'Do you not think we should summon Lizzie?' asked Lady Beverley. 'I know you meant well, Your Grace, but a Beverley does not consort with a mere secretary.'

Miss Trumble raised her eyes to heaven.

'Peter Bond is from an excellent family,' said the duke harshly. Through an open window of the drawing-room which overlooked the side lawn came the sounds of shouts and laughter.

The duke frowned suddenly and went to the window and looked down. Hatless, her red hair glowing like a flame in the sunshine, Lizzie Beverley ran energetically hither and thither. 'I am still better than you, Peter,' she cried gleefully.

And a new Peter, in his shirtsleeves, laughed back.

The duke had meant to punish Lizzie by banishing her from the tea-table. He had not for a moment expected her to look so free, so happy, to have forgotten the very existence of the great Duke of Severnshire. Nor had he expected her to get on such easy terms immediately with his secretary.

'Miss Lizzie, I am sure, would welcome some

24

tea,' he said. He rang the bell and told a footman to tell the young lady that her presence was required.

Lady Beverley had begun to prose on again about Mannerling under the reign of the Beverleys. Miss Trumble watched her nephew curiously as he went back to the window.

The duke waited. He saw the footman call out to Mr Bond. The couple stopped their game. He heard the footman say, 'Your presence is requested by His Grace.'

He quite clearly heard Lizzie say, 'Oh, fiddle, and just when I was beginning to have some fun,' saw the way his secretary's face fell, how he quickly struggled into his black coat and smoothed down his hair.

The duke had never thought about his age before, always somehow thinking of himself as being still a young man. For the first time he felt old and cold and stuffy.

At last he heard them mount the staircase. Lizzie entered, her gloves once more on her hands and her hat on her head. Her face was flushed from the exercise and her eyes shone, but she went meekly to the sofa and sat down primly by her mother – who had not paused for breath – crossed her hands and bowed her head.

She accepted a cup of tea from the footman. Peter bowed to the company, then his master, and made his escape.

The duke sat down and studied Lizzie. She must have been aware of his steady gaze but she calmly drank tea, her long gloves unbuttoned and rolled back over her wrists.

The duke cut right across Lady Beverley's droning monologue. 'Did you enjoy your game, Miss Lizzie?' he asked.

'Yes, I thank you, Your Grace,' said Lizzie meekly.

'The last ball we had here,' said Lady Beverley, ploughing on, 'was a magnificent affair. The footmen had gold swords. I always wondered what happened to those gold swords.'

'They probably went to pay off Papa's debts like most other things,' said Lizzie.

'My dear child,' said Lady Beverley with an icy glare which did not go with the fondness of the words. 'Always funning.'

'My secretary kept you amused, Miss Lizzie?' pursued the duke.

'Yes, I thank you, Your Grace.' Green eyes met silver ones. 'He is most assiduous in attending to his duties, I believe. Does he walk your dogs as well?'

'I did not send you away like a dog,' said the duke sharply.

'I do beg your pardon,' said Lizzie sweetly. 'You were being most kind in thinking I would prefer *young* company.'

'Yes, my dear,' gushed her mother. 'His Grace is kindness itself. But I always think a young lady needs an older man to guide her.'

'How strange, Mama. I would not have thought that at all. Papa was only a year older than you when you married.'

'Ah, but I was old beyond my years. Now you, my dear, are a trifle wayward and flighty, but some gentleman older in years would be able to school you.'

'You forget, Mama, I have the benefit of a superior governess.'

Lady Beverley gave her tinkling laugh. 'Such an innocent!' She smiled at the duke, who gave her a stony look. 'No, no, a husband is something different.'

Lizzie was experiencing an odd feeling of excitement. Mannerling had lost its hold on her. She did not care a whit what this rude duke thought of her. She had forgotten all her good intentions of remaining silent.

'You do not need to worry about a husband for me, Mama, for I am much too plain to fetch one, old or young. As you said yourself, it is a pity I am the runt of the litter.'

The duke covered his mouth with his hand to hide a smile.

'I said no such thing.' Lady Beverley raised a thin white hand to her brow. 'I declare I am feeling a trifle faint. Perhaps some fresh air...?'

Miss Trumble rose to her feet. 'Yes, we must return immediately. I will make you one of my possets, Lady Beverley.' She took Lady Beverley's arm and guided her to the door.

Lizzie curtsied low to the duke. Once more their eyes met and held. Lizzie's green eyes held a mocking, challenging look.

Peter was waiting at the foot of the stairs. 'If you are ever allowed some free time, do call on us,' said Lizzie.

The duke caught the remark as he followed them down the staircase. He was displeased. Lizzie Beverley was a forward, unruly girl.

27

After Barry had helped Lady Beverley into the carriage, then Lizzie, the duke took Miss Trumble aside.

'Even you, Aunt, must admit your pert miss should have watched her tongue.'

'You did, however, send your secretary to take her away for a walk, just like a pet dog,' said Miss Trumble. 'You are annoyed because she dared to enjoy his company. Your trouble, Gervase, is that no one has ever given you a set-down. But what is a little miss like Lizzie to you? You will invite your ladies here to look them over and no doubt you will select one who is as little capable of love and laughter as you are yourself.'

The duke turned on his heel and walked back into the house.

'Your Grace,' said Peter.

'Yes, Mr Bond?'

'The chandelier has begun to move although there is no wind, and I feel a strange air of menace, of threat that seems to come from the very walls.'

The duke stared up at the chandelier as it turned first one way and then the other.

'Vibration from somewhere,' he said curtly. 'And exercise has made you fanciful. I feel nothing.'

He marched up the stairs with his dutiful secretary at his heels.

If a ghost confronted my master, thought Peter, he would probably just order it off the premises!

TWO

Really, if the lower orders don't set us a good example, what on earth is the use of them?

OSCAR WILDE

A week after the tea party found Lady Beverley still confined to her room with one of her imaginary illnesses. 'It is too bad of you, Lizzie,' complained Miss Trumble. 'Your mother always becomes like this when her ambitions are thwarted.'

'They would need to be thwarted in any case,' said Lizzie. 'Better sooner than later.'

'But as I have pointed out, your were impertinent. The duke will invite you to a ball or fête when his guests are in residence and you must behave prettily.'

'He does irritate me,' said Lizzie ruefully.

'Well, we will say no more about it for the moment. Only do try to learn to guard your tongue!'

The duke summoned his secretary and asked if the invitations to his house party had been sent out.

'Yes, Your Grace.'

'Good. That will be all. No, stay. Did you find a young man suitable for Miss Lizzie Beverley?'

'Yes, Your Grace, a certain Mr Gerald Parkes.

Aged twenty and of good family. If you do but remember, we met the young man and his family at Dover last year. Mr Parkes was returning from the Grand Tour. He was all that was amiable and you played backgammon with his father, Colonel Parkes, and thought very highly of him. I took the liberty therefore of inviting Mr Gerald and his parents.'

'That will be all.'

'Very good, Your Grace.'

Peter bowed his way to the door.

'A moment.'

'Yes, Your Grace.'

'You may take tomorrow off. I will not have need of you.'

'Thank you, Your Grace.'

'And if you wish to ride to Hedgefield, say, you may ask the groom to find you a mount.'

'You are very kind, Your Grace.'

'Now you may go.'

Peter closed the double doors of the drawing-room and did a little jig on the landing. He was beginning to detest Mannerling, to find the atmosphere of the great house depressing.

It was indeed a beautiful house, from its painted ceilings to its Persian-carpeted floors. The rooms were gracious and elegantly proportioned. He suddenly thought of Lizzie's invitation and his heart lifted. He would call and pray that Lady Beverley might not find his visit presumptuous.

For some reason, the duke found the memory of Lizzie rankling. She had crossed swords with him and he felt he had somehow lost that first engagement. He had come into his dukedom at an early age. His parents were both dead. Although they had not spent much time with him, they had seen that he had the best of tutors, by which they meant an elderly Scotsman who had toadied to the duke quite dreadfully and the duke had taken that toadying as being exactly what was due to his consequence.

He had attended several Seasons in London in his early twenties, but had not found any female to engage his interest. He had turned his mind to his estates and then in his late twenties to the interests of foreign travel.

He had several people he considered as friends, people that the more ordinary ranks might consider acquaintances, for the duke could not bring himself to confide in anyone. Nor did he feel the need for affection. He had kept several clever and amusing mistresses and when he had tired of them had seen to it that his lawyers had seen each on her way with a generous settlement. When servants became too old to work, they were housed and pensioned.

It was only lately that he had begun to feel a black void in his life. He had justified the purchase of Mannerling to himself by considering it suitable property for an heir, and yet the truth was he had simply felt that this temporary move from his ancestral home might allay his growing ennui.

He felt Lizzie Beverley, she who was supposed to be consumed with ambition to regain Mannerling, had gaily dismissed him as old and boring.

On the following day, as he was walking back to the house after surveying some improvements to the gardens, he saw his secretary ride off down the long drive between the row of lime trees, and knew he was probably going to call at Brookfield House.

He shrugged and turned indoors. It would serve his aunt right if her precious charge became enamoured of a mere secretary.

He decided to get out the carriage and drive over to see old Lady Evans, whom he had once met in London several years before.

His valet laid out his morning coat and breeches and cravat and clean cambric shirt. Once he was dressed, he dismissed his valet and stood in front of the mirror in his room, drawing on his York tan driving gloves.

And suddenly an old man stared back at him from the mirror. It was himself, but horribly aged and stooped. He gasped and covered his face and looked again. But this time only his own well-groomed reflection looked back at him.

Some disorder of the spleen, he thought. The buttered crab last night perhaps had been too rich.

But as he walked down the grand staircase and as two footmen leaped to open the front door for him, he found he was still badly shaken.

His phaeton and horses had been brought round to the front door. He climbed in and picked up the reins. He badly wanted to tell someone what he had seen in the mirror, but winced at the idea of being thought mad.

There were strange stories about Mannerling

being haunted, but he had jeered at all of them.

He drove slowly down the drive, feeling a certain lightness of heart as he reached the lodge-gates. Instead of going to Lady Evans's home, he became convinced that it was his duty to call on his aunt and try once more to persuade her to give up her lowly position in the Beverley household.

Peter found Lizzie in the garden, cutting roses which she laid in a basket on her arm.

'Oh, Peter!' she cried when she saw him. 'You are come. How is it you escaped?'

'His Grace gave me the day off.'

'Do step indoors and I will call Miss Trumble. Mama is lying down.'

'I trust Lady Beverley is not indisposed?'

Lizzie did not want to say that all her mother's ailments were imaginary so she said, 'Mama has the headache but Miss Trumble has given her something for it. Miss Trumble always manages to make Mama feel better.' She laid the basket of roses on a table in the hall.

Miss Trumble came down the stairs. 'Mr Bond,' she said, 'you are welcome.'

Peter felt at ease. Not knowing that Miss Trumble was, in fact, the duke's aunt, he felt on a social level with her.

'But you must have some refreshment,' said Miss Trumble. 'It is such a fine day, it is a pity to waste it indoors. Lizzie, take Mr Bond to the table in the garden and I will tell the maids to bring tea, and see if Josiah has some of his little scones.'

Lizzie's hair was still worn up. She had protested to Miss Trumble that there was no need,
surely, to wear her hair up and be gowned in her
prettiest dresses when no one came to call, but
Miss Trumble said, 'I sent a note to Lady Evans.
She might call at any time. A lady must always
look as if she is expecting callers.'

Lizzie led the way to the table in the garden
under the cedar tree. Peter sat down with a little
sigh of pleasure.

'How fine it is here.'

Lizzie smiled. 'You cannot think it finer than
Mannerling.'

'But I do! I thought you were being fanciful,
Lizzie, when you told me about the chandelier,
but when you left last week, and I entered the
house with my master, the chandelier was turning and there was a brooding air of menace. I
pointed it out to the duke but he dismissed it. He
felt nothing.'

'I think he is probably a very insensitive man.'

'I cannot discuss or criticize my employer,
Lizzie.'

'No, of course you cannot. Here is Miss
Trumble. Miss Trumble, you will think me very
forward, but I have asked Peter here to call me
Lizzie when we are not in company.'

'Be sure you do not let anyone hear you,' said
Miss Trumble reluctantly.

The two maids came out carrying tea, scones
and cakes. Miss Trumble had dismissed them and
was just pouring tea when one of the maids came
running back, the streamers of her cap flying.

'Miss Trumble, my lady wishes to see you.'

Miss Trumble gave a little sigh, but rose obediently to her feet. 'I shall leave Lizzie to entertain you, Mr Bond.'

'So tell me, Peter,' said Lizzie, 'about the duke's plans to marry. He did tell us that those were his plans, so you will not be out of order in talking about them.'

'There is something I can tell you in confidence which shows that my master has considered your future.'

'What can it be?'

'I have invited several people to come on a visit. His Grace asked me to find a suitable young gentleman for you, Lizzie.'

'And have you?'

'Yes, a very pleasant young man. A Mr Gerald Parkes.'

Her eyes flashed. 'That is very high-handed of him to find someone for me. He should have asked me.'

'I think he only meant to be kind.'

'And I think Miss Trumble asked him to find me someone.'

Peter looked surprised. 'Estimable governess as she obviously is, a governess cannot ask a duke to do such a thing.'

'No, I suppose not, Peter,' said Lizzie quickly. 'Tell me about yourself. Are you happy in your employ?'

'I should be.'

'So what is amiss?'

'I would like to tell you, Lizzie, for we are friends, but in my home village, there is a certain lady...'

He blushed and looked down.

'What is her name?' asked Lizzie gently.

'Sarah. Miss Sarah Walters.'

'And is she very fair?'

'Miss Walters has great vivacity and charm. She is Squire Walters's daughter. The family hope for better for her than a mere secretary, even the secretary to a duke. I could not declare myself.'

'How sad.'

'Yes, it is sad. I cannot even write to her.'

Lizzie nodded wisely. It was a world in which one's parents opened and read one's letters first.

'Perhaps,' she said tentatively, 'you might broach the subject to the duke. Who knows? He owns so much property, he might allow you to have a house of your own and sufficient to wed your Sarah.'

Peter gave a mirthless laugh. 'Servants do not marry, as you know very well.'

'I wish there was something I could do for you, Peter.'

He put a hand over hers where it lay on the table and gave it a little squeeze.

The duke, entering the garden, saw what he believed was his secretary holding the hand of Lizzie Beverley in a fond and amorous clasp.

He went straight to the house. The door stood open. 'Miss Trumble!' he called.

Miss Trumble came down the stairs.

'How good of you to call.'

'Come into the parlour,' he said grimly.

Now what? thought Miss Trumble, as he held open the door for her and then shut it firmly behind them.

She sat down, but the duke began to pace up and down. 'Do stand still and tell me what the matter is,' said Miss Trumble.

He ceased his pacing and looked down at her.

'When I arrived, my secretary was sitting in the garden holding hands with Lizzie.'

'Are you sure?'

'Yes, very sure, Aunt. There is something badly wrong when a young miss allows such familiarity and on such short acquaintance.'

'It is all very simple, Gervase. Lizzie, despite her unruly tongue, is not a flirt. We shall go together to the garden and simply ask them what they are about.'

This was the most sensible course and the duke followed her reluctantly out, feeling all the same like a middle-aged gossip.

Peter rose to his feet when he saw his master. Lizzie rose and curtsied. Both young faces were polite blanks and yet the duke sensed he had interrupted something important and that they wished him at the devil.

'We shall all sit down,' said Miss Trumble. 'Lizzie, His Grace was startled, on entering the garden, to see you holding hands with his secretary.'

Peter blushed miserably. 'It was not what you think. There was something troubling me. I told Miss Lizzie and she was so concerned and so understanding that I was moved to cover her hand with my own. Pray accept my apologies.'

'If such be the case,' said Miss Trumble, 'you need not apologize.'

'No, indeed,' said Lizzie. 'But I think you

should tell the duke what it was about. He may be able to help you.'

Peter hung his head.

'Is it something so very dreadful that you fear you might lose your employ?' asked Miss Trumble.

'Oh, no.'

'Tell me about it,' commanded the duke, noticing however the silky sheen of Lizzie Beverley's red hair in the sunlight.

'I am in love,' said Peter wretchedly.

The duke raised his thin eyebrows but said nothing. He simply waited patiently.

'Her name is Sarah Walters,' went on Peter in a low voice. 'She is the daughter of Squire Walters in the village of Syderham, where I grew up. I could not declare my love as I am not in a position to do so. That is all.'

'Does the lady return your affection?' demanded the duke.

'I believe she is not indifferent to me.'

'How old is this village charmer?'

'She will now be eighteen years.'

'And when did you last see Miss Walters?'

'Two years ago.'

'Two years! She may be wed.'

Peter shook his head. 'No, Your Grace. I have a friend in the village who writes to me from time to time. The last letter received was a month ago and Sarah was still unwed. She is very young.'

'May I point out that two years is a long time,' said the duke, 'and in that time Miss Sarah may have changed a great deal. If you put it from your mind, you will forget her.'

'You do not believe in undying love, Your

Grace?' said Lizzie with that mocking note in her voice that irritated him.

'As a matter of fact, I do not believe in love at all,' said the duke.

'It might ease Mr Bond's mind were he allowed time to travel to his village and see for himself,' pointed out Miss Trumble.

'If I recall, Mr Bond lives in Cambridgeshire,' said the duke. 'Too long a journey. I need him here. Besides, secretaries do not marry. Mr Bond knew that very well when he took up the appointment.'

'Why should not secretaries marry?' asked Lizzie. 'Is it because they are supposed to be married to their employers?'

'*Please*, Miss Lizzie,' begged Peter, looking at the duke's hard face.

'Does Miss Walters have brothers and sisters?' asked Miss Trumble.

'She only has one brother, serving in the navy. She had two sisters, younger than she, but they died of cholera.'

'So that is only three – daughter, mother and father,' mused Miss Trumble. 'Mannerling is such a large place and so many rooms. Why, three extra guests at your house party would practically go unnoticed.'

The duke was aware of a pair of mocking green eyes on his face waiting for him to give Miss Trumble a set-down.

'Yes, why not,' he said, locking eyes with Lizzie. 'Mr Bond, you may send out an invitation to Squire Walters and his family.'

'Oh, Your Grace. How can I ever thank you?'

'By not letting your unrequited passion interfere with your work,' said the duke acidly.

'Oh, now that is settled,' said Lizzie, clapping her hands, 'would you care for a game of croquet?'

Mr Bond looked at the duke who said, 'It is your free day. You may do as you wish.'

'We will all play,' said Miss Trumble.

What should have been an amiable and friendly game became a serious contest when it became clear that Lizzie and the duke were determined to beat each other.

At last Lizzie won and danced around the lawn, waving her mallet in the air and crying, 'I beat you! I beat you!'

'Unruly child,' admonished Miss Trumble. 'Let us repair indoors and have some luncheon. The exercise will have given us an appetite.'

The duke hesitated. He felt he had lowered himself by playing croquet with a noisy hoyden and his own secretary. And yet a feeling that they would all enjoy themselves immensely once he had gone made him say, 'How kind.'

When they were seated round the dining-table, the duke said, 'Does Lady Beverley know I am here?'

'I did not tell her,' said Miss Trumble. 'Lady Beverley is not well and she should not be disturbed by any excitement.'

Peter would normally have been shy at sitting down to a meal with his employer, but Lizzie began to chat about the latest letters she had received from her sisters and how happy they all were and Miss Trumble began to tease the duke, saying that Lizzie's sisters' happiness all went to prove that love was a necessary ingredient in a marriage.

'These are unusual cases,' said the duke loftily. 'For my part, I have found that an arranged marriage between suitable parties is the only recipe for success.'

'You mean,' said Lizzie, 'that some lady will marry you for your title and fortune and you will marry her for her good family and her dowry. What of passion?'

The duke looked shocked. 'Passion is an emotion of the lower orders. Ladies do not feel passion.'

'Oh yes, they do,' said Miss Trumble quietly.

The duke became angry. 'Really, Aunt, it is surely your duty to instill more ladylike thoughts into the mind of your charge.'

'Aunt?' Peter looked bewildered.

'I regret to tell you that Miss Trumble is in fact my aunt, Lady Letitia Revine,' said the duke, 'and I do order you to keep that fact to yourself. She has adopted the ridiculous name of Trumble and will be addressed as such until this farce is over.'

'And when will that be?'

'When Lizzie is married,' put in Miss Trumble.

'Then that should not be very long,' said Peter. 'Miss Lizzie's looks and charm will break hearts.'

Lizzie sent him a roguish, teasing look. 'Why, you are a gallant!'

Peter laughed. He had lost his careworn look. The thought that he would soon see his Sarah again bubbled through his veins like champagne.

His gaiety was infectious. Lizzie chattered on,

41

Miss Trumble smiled, and the duke felt an odd longing to be part of all this happiness.

After lunch, Miss Trumble suggested they play cards. 'No, no,' protested Lizzie. 'The day is too fine for cards. Let's play hide-and-seek.'

The duke opened his mouth to wither such a suggestion. But Miss Trumble said, 'Why not? Except anywhere upstairs is out of bounds in case we disturb Lady Beverley. I know. The garden.'

'I should take my leave,' said the duke.

'Is it a game you are not good at?' asked Lizzie sweetly.

'It is a game I have not played since I was in short coats.'

'Perhaps it is a trifle too young and energetic for you, Gervase,' said Miss Trumble, taking pity on him.

In his mind's eye, the duke suddenly saw that terrible reflection in the mirror at Mannerling. 'I think it might amuse me,' he said languidly.

They drew straws and the duke found he was the one to count to a hundred. They left him sitting at the table under the cedar-tree with his hands over his eyes while they all scattered away across the garden.

Miss Trumble went straight to the tack-room, where she knew she would find Barry polishing the harness.

'So the great duke has come on a visit,' said Barry. 'You all sound very merry.'

'I am supposed to be playing hide-and-seek,' said Miss Trumble, sitting down on a battered chair with a sigh of relief. 'I am amazed Gervase elected to play. I cannot be bothered hiding.'

'Has Miss Lizzie been rude to the duke?'

'She mocks him.'

'You must curb her tongue, miss!'

'I think it does him good. Gervase needs to be shocked out of some of his arrogance. And yet, why does he stay? See, here he comes and I am sure he has glimpsed me through the tack-room window for the flowers on my bonnet are quite bright, and yet I know he will pass here and go in search of his real quarry, which is Lizzie. No, he is not enamoured of her by any means. He simply cannot bear to be mocked and to that end he will pursue her until he considers she has a fitting respect for his greatness.'

The sun was very warm. The duke decided, as he had appeared to have forgotten the conventions this day, he may as well forget them further. He took off his blue swallow-tailed coat and hung it on a fence-post. A pleasant breeze ruffled the fine cambric sleeves of his shirt. Where would that minx Lizzie hide?

As he approached the small stable and tack-room, he saw a bright flash of yellow at the tack-room window. Miss Trumble had yellow silk flowers on her hat. He veered away. He did not want to find Miss Trumble.

He wandered through the gardens, looking to right and left. If I were a hoyden like Lizzie Beverley, where would I hide? He answered his own question. In a tree, of course.

He began to look up in the branches of the trees. She was wearing a white muslin gown. At the southern end of the garden, marking its boundary, was a small stream. On the other side of the stream was a large oak tree with wide spreading branches. His eye caught a glimmer of white among the shifting leaves.

He smiled and strode across the flat stepping-stones in the stream.

He stood under the tree and looked up. 'You are discovered, Miss Lizzie.'

The leaves above him parted and her face looked down. 'Fiddle,' said Miss Lizzie Beverley crossly.

'Come down,' he commanded.

A pair of neat ankles came into view. She slipped, and missed her footing. He caught her in his arms as she fell, feeling for one moment her soft pliant body against his own. A strand of that red, silky hair had come loose from its pins and blew across his mouth.

'Have you found Mr Bond?' asked Lizzie when he had set her on her feet.

'Neither Mr Bond nor Miss Trumble.'

'Then you must play properly.'

'Very well. For your information, Miss Trumble is in the tack-room and Mr Bond is behind the hedge at the front of the garden, which is cheating because that is out on the road.'

'But if you did not tell them they had been seen, then they may have moved somewhere else.'

'Possibly. Let us go and see.'

'How clever of you to find me,' said Miss Trumble when they opened the tack-room door. And Mr Bond, when called, came sheepishly out from behind the hedge.

'Now it is your turn, Lizzie,' said Miss Trumble.

Lizzie obediently sat down at the table and covered her eyes. When she uncovered them and looked up, it was to find her mother standing there. 'The duke's carriage is outside. His crest is on the panel,' said Lady Beverley. 'Why was I not informed, and what are you doing here with your hair in a mess and leaves in your gown?'

'We are playing hide-and-seek, Mama.'

'Who is "we"?'

'The duke, his secretary, Miss Trumble, and me.'

'What will he think of such inelegant behaviour?'

'He is playing as well, Mama,' said Lizzie patiently. 'I must go and find him and the others. You were not informed of his visit because you are unwell.'

'I shall wait here,' said Lady Beverley crossly. 'But when this stupid game is over, go inside and get Betty to tidy your hair and change your gown.'

Lizzie ran off. She quickly discovered Miss Trumble, only half-hidden by a bush. Peter had decided to change his hiding-place from behind the corner of the house to a bush opposite and Lizzie caught him as he ran across.

'Now for your master,' she said.

She searched diligently in all her own hiding places without success. Where on earth could he be? He was so tall. Where would he hide?

Where would he expect her *not* to look for him?

She smiled suddenly. She was sure he would hide where she had hidden herself, being sure she would never think of looking there.

Lizzie made her way through the garden, over the stepping-stones, and stood under the oak tree.

'Come down!' she called.

She could not possibly see him, he thought. He had climbed to the topmost branches, those that could bear his weight, and knew he was well-screened by thick leaves. It was childish, but he wanted to win the game.

And then he heard her begin to climb. She cannot climb this far up, he thought. But he heard a rustling in the leaves and branches until, like an elfin jack-in-the-box, her head popped through the screen of leaves and she grinned up at him. 'Caught, Your Grace. Well and truly caught.'

'Very well, you win,' he capitulated. 'I trust you can get down.'

'Easily,' said Lizzie. She peered down through the branches and gave a little gasp of fright. The ground seemed to be a terribly long way away. Her head disappeared but then her shaky voice reached his ears. 'I cannot. I am stuck.'

He cautiously left his perch and edged down. 'You will stand on me!' screeched Lizzie.

He looked down on her red head.

'I will slide down onto that branch next to you and then you must hold very tightly around my neck and I will carry you down.'

He cautiously manoeuvred himself down onto a branch next to her. 'Now lean across, you silly widgeon, and put your arms around my neck.'

He turned his back on her and waited while he heard her edging closer and then felt her arms go round him.

'Do not let go!' He picked his way from branch to branch, aware of the young body pressed so close against his own.

When he finally set her down, Lizzie found she was trembling. In an age when a chaste kiss or a pressure of the hand was the most young ladies received from their gentlemen before marriage, the intimate pressure of his hard-muscled body seemed stamped all over hers, that it had some-how *invaded* hers. And yet as he took her hand and helped her over the stepping-stones once more, he was all that was correct.

'You have found the others?' he asked.

'Yes, easily.'

'I have been forgetting the real reason for my visit.'

'Which is?'

'To persuade my aunt to end this undignified farce.'

'Miss Trumble – for I will always think of her as that – is a dedicated teacher and that has more nobility about it than leading the life of an unwanted maiden aunt.'

'She has forgotten what is due to her position.'

'The Beverleys were well-nigh on the road to ruining themselves because of arrogance. Miss Trumble has escaped all that.'

'You are a radical!'

'If being a radical means having a modicum of common sense, then I am.'

He looked down at her, irritated. He felt she should be more in awe of him, instead of talking to him in this direct manner.

And yet he would have stayed, and he would have gladly played another game, had he not seen Lady Beverley sitting waiting for him, and then all he could think of was making his escape.

Peter, also, said he must leave.

'You may come with me in my carriage, Mr Bond,' said the duke. 'We will tether your horse to the back.'

After they made their goodbyes and set off for Mannerling, the duke said, 'Instruct the servants to remove the mirror from my room and replace it with another. The glass is very old and does not give a true reflection.'

At the breakfast table the following day, the Earl of Hernshire read his post, finally arriving at the duke's invitation. 'Here's a thing,' he cried. 'We are invited by Severnshire to go on a visit. He has bought a new property, Mannerling.'

His countess looked up from her morning paper in surprise. 'What does he want with a new property? Has that palace of his burnt down?'

'It does not say.' The earl rattled the stiff parchment of the letter. 'You know what this invitation means, Verity?'

His daughter put down her cup of chocolate and said calmly, 'He is thinking of choosing me for a wife.'

The earl gave a little sigh. He could not understand why Verity was still unwed. Her three younger sisters had all married well. And yet, here was Verity, the flower of them all, still a spinster at the great age of twenty-five. She had masses of thick brown hair, large liquid brown eyes, a patrician nose and a small mouth. Her bust was good, her neck was long. Her ankles and legs were thick but always concealed in long gowns. She had received three proposals of marriage but had

48

turned them all down, saying they were not good enough for her.

'If he does propose,' said the earl sharply, 'I hope you will not turn all haughty and refuse him.'

'Of course not,' said Verity. 'He *is* a duke, after all.'

In a neighbouring county, the Charter family were exclaiming over the duke's invitation to them. 'Oh, Celia,' said her fond mother. 'A duke, no less.'

Celia was small and fair-haired with large round blue eyes in a plump face. Her nose was unfortunate, being small and upturned, but she had a dainty little figure and neat ankles. She had only attended one Season and was popular enough but had set her cap at a baron, and the baron had heartlessly proposed to her best friend, Emily, and been accepted. So for her parents, the expensive Season had been a waste of money. Now, from the duke's letter, it looked as if they might not have to waste money on another Season. The duke had not met Celia, and yet had invited her, and that could only mean one thing: marriage!

'You will have a great household and many servants to command,' warned her father, 'and you must show yourself up to the task. Severnshire is very grand. Do not be familiar with the servants.'

'I am never familiar with servants,' said Celia, and then ran upstairs to discuss the prospects of this exciting invitation with her lady's-maid.

English squires are always pictured as being bluff and hearty, but Squire Walters was old and wizened and penny-pinching. He did not even hunt, considering the keeping of horses and hounds an unnecessary expenditure. His wife, Mrs Walters, was twenty years younger than he, a small, crushed woman whose faded looks still held traces of earlier beauty.

'Dukes do not court ladies, they select them,' said the squire, rubbing his hands, which gave off a dry rustling sound like mating snakes. 'He has heard of our Sarah's beauty and has selected her. If she does not take, we will, however, endeavour to stay as long as possible, for the saving on coals and candles alone will be immense.'

Mrs Walters said nothing. She had learned the hard way to open her mouth as little as possible, for the squire took great delight in criticizing her and finding fault.

Sarah Walters said nothing either. She spent her days in dreams, dreams which shut out the angry voice of her father, which usually only came to her as an irritating buzz, such as a trapped wasp makes.

But she had heard that she was invited to be a guest of the Duke of Severnshire and immediately became locked in a really splendid dream. She would escape from her mother and father at last. She would be a duchess and have all the pretty dresses her heart craved. She would dine from gold plates. Liveried footmen would follow her everywhere, carrying her parcels when she shopped for luxuries. She would keep a parrot and train it to say, 'Beautiful Sarah.'

She was a slight, black-haired girl with very white skin and grey eyes. Her nose was a trifle long, but that was no disadvantage in an age when to have a little nose was damned as vulgar. The fact that her meagre wardrobe only contained unfashionable gowns did not trouble her. The duke must somehow have seen her one day, and the arrow of love had pierced his heart. He would be broad and strong with hair as black as her own and a tanned face. He would be friendly and kind.

'How hard your life has been, my beauty,' he would murmur. 'Be mine, and I will cherish and protect you for the rest of your life.'

She frowned a little as a half-remembered face intruded into her dream, that of a young man. Oh, it was that nice Mr Bond who had left the village. There was some connection there with the duke but she could not remember what it was.

One morning, Lady Beverley summoned Miss Trumble. 'I have decided to go to Bath. I am in need of restorative waters.'

'Do you wish that I and Lizzie should accompany you?'

'I may send for you,' said Lady Beverley. 'I am quite cast down and wish to get away. I had great hopes, great hopes after the duke's arrival. But Lizzie spoilt everything. What she lacks in looks, she could have made up for by being modest and correct. But, no, she must run about the garden playing childish games and give the duke a disgust of her. Mannerling is lost to us forever. Whatever did I do to have such undutiful daughters? I will need a post-chaise, and Barry and the maid, Betty, must accompany me.'

'I will tell Barry to ride over to Hedgefield and

51

arrange the hire of a post-chaise,' said Miss Trumble.

In Miss Trumble's pocket was a letter from the duke which had arrived only that morning. In it, he had requested that his aunt, Lady Beverley and Lizzie join his house party. Miss Trumble had no intention of letting Lady Beverley see that letter. She could go to Bath and therefore relieve Lizzie of the awful social embarrassment of hearing her mother prose on about the Beverleys and Mannerling.

'I shall leave on Saturday,' said Lady Beverley.

And we are expected at Mannerling on Friday, thought Miss Trumble. A day late will not matter. But she must not find out we are going.

'Was that not a servant from Mannerling I saw this morning?' asked Lady Beverley.

'Yes, he brought a letter to me from my nephew.'

'Did he mention me?'

'No, he did not.'

Lady Beverley sighed. It was all very awkward having Miss Trumble revealed as an aristocrat. Miss Trumble had even stopped addressing her as 'my lady.' But Lady Beverley could hardly correct her for that or she herself might have to begin to address Miss Trumble as my lady.

'Lizzie has ruined everything,' she mourned. 'There is nothing left for me to do but to take my failing health to Bath. What is it, Betty?'

'Mrs Judd is called to see you.'

'I will tell her you are not at home,' said Miss Trumble quickly. Mary Judd, the vicar's daughter, had trounced Lady Beverley's ambitions in the past by marrying a previous owner of Mannerling.

But Judd had run into gambling debts and had hanged himself from the chandelier in the Great Hall, and Mary had never quite got over having to return to the vicarage and live again with her father.

'I will see her,' said Lady Beverley.

In truth, Lady Beverley rather enjoyed Mary's company, for Mary toadied to her and Lady Beverley interpreted such toadying as a due respect to her rank. It would have shocked the Duke of Severnshire to know that he had that much in common with Lady Beverley.

Mary was in the parlour, dressed as usual in black. Some gentleman two years after the death of her husband had said she looked very well in black and so Mary had worn it ever since.

'Lady Beverley,' she said, dropping a full court curtsy. 'I am indeed honoured that you can spare me some time.'

'I have always time for you,' said Lady Beverley, advancing and giving her two fingers to shake.

'Have you met the Duke of Severnshire?' asked Mary, although she knew very well from local gossip that the duke had called at Brookfield House.

'Yes, we were invited to tea and he was a guest here.'

'And unmarried!' said Mary slyly. 'Has he shown any signs of being taken by Lizzie?'

'Lizzie,' said Lady Beverley, 'is a wayward child who has given him a disgust of her. If only it had been one of her other sisters – Isabella, for example – whose beauty was unsurpassed. I shall be leaving at the end of the week, Mary.'

'To London?' Mary pronounced it the old-fashioned way – Lunnon.

'No, to Bath. I am frail. No one understands how delicate my nerves are.'

'You are a brave lady, and have come through many tribulations with fortitude,' said Mary. 'I have long admired you. Ah, Bath. The elegant buildings, the walks, the Pump Room, how I would love to see it all one day.'

'Then you shall,' said Lady Beverley on sudden impulse. 'If your father can do without you, then you may come as my companion.'

Her father would just need to do without her, thought Mary. 'I consider it a great honour and a great privilege.'

And Lady Beverley, who quibbled about the very price of coal for the fires in winter, was quite happy to open the purse-strings to play Lady Bountiful to this daughter of the vicarage who knew her place so well, when others did not.

Miss Trumble told Lizzie in private about the invitation, explaining that it would be wise to keep her mother in happy ignorance.

'I wish we did not have to go,' said Lizzie.

'Why?'

'Peter told me the duke had found a beau for me. Was that your idea?'

'Yes, it was. Do not look so downcast, Lizzie. You are not expected to marry the fellow. I merely thought that someone cheerful and closer to your own age might amuse you.'

'But there is Peter.'

'Mr Bond will be so taken up with his duties and gazing on his beloved that he will have no

54

time for you.'

'Mama will be furious when she finds out.'

'We will see to it she does not. Do you know, she has asked that creature, Mary Judd, to accompany her to Bath?'

'But I thought she had never forgiven Mary for marrying Judd.'

'Well, you know how Mary toadies and Lady Beverley's spirit is badly bruised these days. Your mother does not know quite how to go on with me and she blames your hoydenish games for disaffecting the duke when I fear it was the very sight of her and the dread of hearing more tales of the Beverleys' days of greatness which drove him away.'

Lizzie looked at her governess sharply. 'I hope you, my sensible Miss Trumble, do not entertain any hopes of my catching the duke.'

'You are much too young,' said Miss Trumble dismissively. 'I doubt if Gervase is even aware of you as a young lady.'

Lizzie went to her room and sat down in front of the mirror. She was wearing her hair down. A schoolgirl looked back at her. She swept up her hair on top of her head. She was not interested in the duke. Not she! But the fact that he might be totally unaware of her as a young lady rankled.

Thanks to the generosity of her elder married sisters, she now had a wardrobe of pretty and fashionable clothes.

She would make an effort to be as mondaine and charming as possible.

No one, not even a duke, should be unaware of the presence of such as Lizzie Beverley!

THREE

The young ladies entered the drawing-room in the full fervour of sisterly animosity.

R. S. SURTEES

Miss Trumble had sent a reply to the duke, saying that Lady Beverley would be in Bath, but that she and Lizzie accepted his invitation. Perhaps he would be so good as to send a carriage for them?

'For Barry will be gone,' explained Miss Trumble to Lizzie, 'and we can hardly arrive at such a grand affair driving the carriage ourselves.'

Lady Beverley was waved goodbye, the post-chaise laden down with luggage which included a large trunk full of patent medicines. As the carriage moved off, Mary turned and gave Lizzie a triumphant little smirk which showed Mary thought she was the favoured one, with the daughter being left behind.

There is going to be the most awful scene when Mama finds out we went to Mannerling without her, thought Lizzie.

The two maids were busy packing her clothes. Lizzie felt a twinge of apprehension and could not understand it. She had met very grand company in London, her sisters were all married to rich and important men. But she had always been the youngest, a looker-on of her sisters' love tangles. If she did not find a man to marry, then Miss

56

Trumble could not stay forever and so she would be left in the country with only her mother for company.

What would this young man be like, this Gerald Parkes? Probably callow and dull and only wanting to talk about himself while he expected her to simper.

The day they set out for Mannerling was hot and close and still. Dry little leaves rustled down from the trees beside the road, a sort of false autumn.

Lizzie could not understand why her feelings of apprehension would not go away. She wished they had been able to arrive on the same day as the other guests. Now they would all be established and have got to know each other. As the newcomers, they would be studied and assessed. Her broad-brimmed straw Hat held a whole garden of flowers, the latest fashion, sent from London by her sister Abigail. Her morning gown of Brussels lace was all the crack, sent by her sister Rachel. Miss Trumble had dressed her hair up in the latest style. If only she felt elegant inside!

The carriage bowled smoothly up the long straight drive to the porticoed entrance of Mannerling. But there was no longer a quickening of the heart at the thought of going 'home'. For the very first time, Lizzie thought of Brookfield House as home, and wished heartily she were back there, sitting in the stables, talking to Barry.

But Barry Wort had gone to Bath with her mother. Certainly, he would be sent back as soon as the journey was completed. Although Barry often acted as footman on special occasions for the Beverleys in a second-hand suit of red plush and a glass wig, Lady Beverley was ashamed of him. Footmen should be slim, six feet tall, and haughty.

As Lizzie had noticed before, the duke seemed to have a great many servants. As the carriage drew to a stop, two tall footmen, who would have gladdened Lady Beverley's heart, jumped down from the back-strap to let down the steps. Other footmen began to unload their luggage. Butler and housekeeper followed them up to their rooms, and soon they were surrounded by a flurry of maids unpacking their luggage.

Lizzie found she was in her old bedroom with its adjoining private sitting-room. She walked around examining everything. The old four-poster bed in which she used to sleep had been replaced by a modern one with a canopy from which lace bed-curtains descended. In the sitting-room, there was new furniture, gilt with striped silk upholstery in green and gold. The wallpaper was of a green-and-gold Chinese pattern. The clock over the mantel, the little gilt French clock, was the same, as was the escritoire in the corner. How awful it had been, she remembered, when Papa's debts had been so great that they could not even remove some of their favourite pieces of furniture. Mannerling no longer reached out to her.

It was mid-afternoon. Miss Trumble entered and said, 'We are to join the company in the drawing-room for tea. Let me see to your hair.'

Lizzie obediently went into her bedroom and sat down at the toilet-table. 'This is my old room,

Miss Trumble,' she said. 'But some things are different. Even this mirror is different. I remember it now. It is a very old one and used to be in Papa's dressing-room.'

'The glass gives a good reflection,' said Miss Trumble, adjusting bone-pins amongst the curls and coils of red hair. 'You will do very well, Lizzie.'

'I am now anxious to see Peter's beloved,' said Lizzie. 'Is she here?'

'I gather from a footman that everyone is arrived.'

As they walked together along the corridor and down the stairs to the drawing-room, Lizzie felt her heart begin to beat hard and wondered if an actor felt like this just before he made his appearance on the stage.

Two footmen sprang to open the double doors and they entered.

Eyes, eyes, eyes everywhere, staring and assessing.

The duke moved forward. 'May I present Miss Lizzie Beverley and my ... and Miss Trumble.'

Both curtsied. The duke led them round the room while Lizzie tried to remember who was who. The Chumleys, Mr and Mrs, round and comfortable-looking. The Earl and Countess of Hernshire; the earl, small and tubby, the countess, tall and stately. Daughter, Lady Verity, with a chilly smile, turning indifferently away as soon as the introductions had been made.

Then the Charters – as silly as their silly little daughter, thought Miss Trumble.

Squire Walters, his wife, and daughter Sarah.

They came as a great disappointment to Lizzie. The squire was wizened and nasty-looking, his wife frightened, and his daughter so vague and dreamy that she did not quite seem to know where she was.

Next was Colonel Parkes, genial and courteous, with a jolly, friendly wife.

And son, Gerald.

Lizzie blinked up at him in a dazed way. He was a young Adonis. Hair as gold as the sun and eyes as blue as a summer sea. His face was lightly tanned and very, very handsome.

Lizzie smiled at him and curtsied.

'The formalities seem to be over,' said Gerald, looking down at Lizzie. He grinned and the duke moved away, feeling obscurely that he had been banished. Tea was served. Lady Verity and Celia Charter were seated on a backless sofa on either side of the duke. Verity was trying to catch his attention, but Celia was prattling away, ogling and flirting, while her parents looked on with approval. Sarah Walters was holding a teacup halfway to her lips and gazing dreamily out of the window. Her father kept darting her vicious little looks, as if he would like to slap her back into the real world.

Gerald and Lizzie were seated side by side on another sofa. The rest of the house party were assembled on chairs, balancing cake plate and teacup while sitting up rigidly straight. Only commoners allowed their bodies to touch the back of the chair.

'I really did not want to come,' confided Gerald.

'Why not?' asked Lizzie.

'Look about you, Miss Lizzie. I am quite out-shone by Severnshire. Every lady wants to become a duchess.'

'Not I!' said Lizzie.

'Why not? You would make a very pretty little duchess.'

'Thank you, sir.'

'Like a Dresden figurine.'

'You put me to the blush. May I remind you that Dresden figurines do not have red hair.'

'They should have hair like yours. But now I think of it, they are too insipid-coloured. Your hair is like a flame, like a glorious autumn, like a winter sunset.'

'I beg you to stop,' cried Lizzie. 'I am not in the way of receiving compliments, and my head will be quite turned if you go on.'

'Then we will talk of prosaic things. Did you have a long journey to get here?'

'Not at all. I live hard by. In fact, my family once lived here.'

'Of course. Beverley. The Beverleys of Mannerling. I have heard of your family. Your sisters all married great men. You have been lying to me, Miss Lizzie. You must want to outshine your sisters and become a duchess.'

'Not I! Severnshire is very grim, I think, and quite old.'

'You are too hard. We first met him at Dover. My parents had come to meet me after my return from the Grand Tour. He was all that was amiable.'

'I should think anyone would feel amiable with your parents around,' said Lizzie, noticing the

61

way that Colonel and Mrs Parkes were chatting happily with Miss Trumble.

'Who is that lady you came in with?'

'That is Miss Trumble. She was my governess but I suppose she is now my chaperone. Mama is in Bath taking the waters.'

'Miss Trumble looks much too grand to be anyone's governess. Her gown is of the first stare. Lady Beverley must be a generous employer.'

But Lizzie did not want to go on talking about Miss Trumble in case she betrayed that lady's identity.

Peter hovered nervously outside the drawing-room. He had not seen Sarah since her arrival. He had been sent into Gloucester the day before when she arrived to attend to business. That had involved leaving at dawn and not arriving back until everyone else was in bed.

He longed to see her. He had a letter in his hand for the duke which had arrived that morning. It concerned a boundary dispute on the duke's home estates. He was quite well able to deal with the matter himself, but in his longing to see Sarah again he had persuaded himself that his master would want to attend to it personally.

At last he smoothed his hair and squared his shoulders and walked into the drawing-room. Everyone looked at him. Peter's eyes flew straight to Sarah. She looked vaguely at him, a little frown creasing her brow, and then she retreated back into her dream in which the duke was proposing marriage to her. The fact that she had made not the slightest push to attract the duke's attention did not strike her as ridiculous. Sarah preferred dreams to reality. In dreams people were always charming and said all the things one wanted them to say.

The duke rose, interrupting Celia's prattle and said, 'Mr Bond. You have something for me?'

They walked to a corner of the drawing-room. Peter handed him the letter. The duke read it with surprise. He was about to say sharply that Mr Bond should be able to cope with the matter himself when he noticed how nervous the young man was. 'Mr and Mrs Walters,' said the duke, raising his voice. 'Do you not recognize Mr Bond? He is from your village.'

'What?' The squire peered at Peter. Sarah continued to look out of the window where her wedding breakfast was taking place in marquees on the lawn. The duke in his wedding clothes was standing at her side. They were receiving the best wishes of the tenantry.

'Oh, yes, Bond's son,' said the squire. 'Dead, ain't he?'

'Yes, Mr Walters,' said Peter. 'My father died just before I took up my post with His Grace.'

'Glad you're settled,' mumbled the squire. 'Bond didn't leave you anything.'

'Miss Walters!' said the duke in a commanding voice.

Sarah came back to earth and blinked at him. 'Do you remember Mr Bond?'

Her eyes focused at last on Peter. 'Why, of course,' she said. 'You danced with me at the local assembly. How are you?'

'Very well,' said Peter.

There was a silence. Then Miss Trumble said, 'I am sure you must have much to talk about. Mr Bond, why do you not sit with Miss Walters for a little?'

Celia Charter goggled at Miss Trumble and Verity said acidly, 'Whether his secretary stays or not is a matter for the duke, not for a local governess.'

'I will go,' said Peter wretchedly.

'No, Mr Bond, you must not let the bad manners of one of my guests drive you away. Pray be seated,' said the duke.

Lizzie looked at Verity, wondering how she was liking that set-down, but she heard Verity say to Celia, 'I hope that puts that uppity governess in her place for once and for all. She *was* rude.'

'Apart from us,' said Gerald cheerfully, 'it's a pretty horrible guest-list. Only look how the squire glares at that young secretary.'

Sarah was enjoying herself, talking about village matters. The fact that Peter was adoringly hanging on her every word went unnoticed by her.

'How do you think our host plans to entertain us today?' Gerald went on. 'Or will he bother? After tea, we will all repair to our rooms and rest from the rigours of raising a cup to our lips.'

'I have no suggestions,' said Lizzie. 'I am resolved to be correct.'

Gerald's blue eyes sparkled with mischief.

'And what would you do were you not being correct?'

'I would probably go out into the sunshine and walk about the gardens and look around all my favourite old haunts.'

'Why do you not show them to me? Leave this fusty, musty tea-party?'

'I think Miss Trumble would consider it proper to escort me.'

'Surely not! In broad daylight, in the gardens, in full view of anyone who might care to see you?'

'Nonetheless, I will ask her,' said Lizzie.

She rose and crossed to Miss Trumble, who looked up inquiringly. 'Mr Parkes and I would like to take a turn around the gardens in the sunshine, Miss Trumble.'

Miss Trumble hesitated only a second. She glanced at Mr and Mrs Parkes, who were smiling their approval.

'Yes, by all means, Lizzie,' she said. 'But do not stray too far from the house.'

The duke saw them leave. He then turned away and looked at the window. But the sun was still shining. Odd. He could have sworn the room had become suddenly darker.

'Oof! That's better,' exclaimed Gerald as they emerged from the darkness of the hall and out into the sunlight. 'I am not made for the social life.'

Lizzie looked amused. 'And what are you made for, Mr Parkes?'

'I am made for adventure, excitement. I think I shall join the army. Do you not get bored with all this social chit-chat among the teacups, Miss Lizzie?'

'I usually lead a very quiet life, Mr Parkes. I have not travelled. Only to London, and that does not count. So a visit to my old home and meeting new people is a welcome diversion.'

'I like the sights and smells of foreign countries,' said Gerald. 'Oh, the sunshine in Italy. We will probably remember this fine summer when we are quite old because it is so unusual. But in Italy the sun shines every day and there is a restless, excited feeling in the streets.'

'What of the art and architecture?'

'Oh, those. Well, people do prose on and drag on about the churches and ruins, but it was the life in the streets which interested me. You should see Venice, Miss Lizzie. Streets of water with the sun shining on it like molten gold.'

'It is very fine here,' said Lizzie primly, 'and you have not looked about you once.'

'I was looking at your enchanting face.'

'You are trying to make me fall in love with you, sir, and all for your amusement.'

Gerald, who had been hoping for a flirtatious dalliance with this little redhead to beguile the tedium of a country visit, burst out laughing, and said, 'Are you usually so perceptive?'

'On the contrary, I often do not see what is under my very nose. Let me just say your tactics make your motives very plain.'

'You do not have much vanity, do you, Miss Lizzie? Many a lady would have believed every word I said.'

'They can't have had red hair,' said Lizzie gloomily.

'Silly fashions. They come and go. You will make red hair the fashion.'

'I am not fashionable, either in looks or speech.'

'That is what makes you so intriguing.'

'There you go again,' said Lizzie on a sigh. 'Let

us walk to the folly and look at the lake.'

'So we walk to the folly and look at the lake, and then what?'

'It is a very beautiful view,' said Lizzie reprovingly.

He laughed and strode out in the direction of the lake so that she had to scamper, holding on to her hat, to keep up with him.

'The view will not go away,' she panted.

He slowed his step and smiled down at her. Lizzie felt suddenly a little breathless and it was nothing to do with the fast pace. Gerald Parkes was so very beautiful.

'You look startled. What's amiss?' he asked.

'You are very beautiful.'

'And you are bamming me!'

'Oh, dear,' said Lizzie, colouring up. 'I have spoken my mind again. How embarrassing. I beg you to forget it.'

'Not I! I shall preen myself quite dreadfully for the rest of the day.'

'Be sensible. Now here is the folly. Mr Judd, the owner of Mannerling who hanged himself, blew it up. This is a replacement.'

'He must have been all about in his upper chambers. Why did he blow it up?'

'He had taken the Beverleys in dislike. He knew that he was expected to marry Isabella, my eldest sister, and he let her believe he meant to propose at the first ball he held at Mannerling. Instead, he proposed to the vicar's daughter.'

'What a truly dreadful man. Would your sister have really married him just to regain Mannerling?'

Lizzie bit her lip. 'It seems a madness now. We felt we were nobodies without Mannerling. Our pride and ambition were great. But Isabella fell deeply in love with Lord Fitzpatrick and so it all had a happy ending.'

'For everyone – except Mr Judd.'

The sunlight sparkled on the lake, where two brightly coloured rowing-boats held by their painters bobbed beside a small wooden jetty. Weeping willows trailed long fingers in the still water.

'If you want excitement,' said Lizzie, 'you should go and look down into the waters of the lake when they are still and clear as they are today. People have seen the drowned face of Mr Cater.'

'And who was Mr Cater? Another suicidal owner?'

'No, but he wished to possess Mannerling. He disappeared from our lives and we never found out what became of him.'

'I have never seen a ghost,' cried Gerald. 'Let's go and look.'

'Not I,' said Lizzie with a shudder. 'I believe in ghosts.'

With a laugh, he ran lightly down the grassy bank which led to the jetty. He turned and waved to Lizzie. When he reached the jetty, he knelt down on one knee and stared down into the water.

Lizzie waited and watched anxiously.

Then she heard Gerald cry out, saw him clutch his throat, then he fell back on the jetty and lay prone, his hat rolling off into the water.

'Mr Parkes!' screamed Lizzie.

She ran headlong down to the jetty and knelt down beside him, rubbing his wrists and cheeks. 'Please, Mr Parkes,' she begged. 'Do not be dead.'

His blue eyes suddenly opened and he said, 'I think a kiss would restore me to life.'

'Monster!' Lizzie got to her feet and glared down at him.

'I fooled you,' he cried gleefully, springing to his feet. 'You should see your face.'

Lizzie turned and began to walk angrily away. 'I will never forgive you,' she said over her shoulder.

The duke, irritated by Celia and bored with Verity, stood once more at the drawing-room window.

His eyes narrowed. There was Lizzie Beverley, hurrying back towards the house. Gerald Parkes was following her He seemed to be pleading. Then, as the duke watched, Gerald ran around the front of Lizzie and sank to his knees and clasped his hands.

He saw Lizzie begin to laugh, saw Gerald get to his feet with a sunny smile and tuck Lizzie's hand in his arm. Chatting together, they continued towards the house.

Mr Bond has done well for that chit, thought the duke sourly.

Lizzie and Gerald entered the hall. Suddenly Lizzie stopped.

'What is the matter?' asked Gerald.

'The house is angry with me,' whispered Lizzie.

'I beg your pardon?'

'Nothing,' said Lizzie, 'nothing at all.'

She ran away from him and up the stairs.

How odd, thought Gerald. She was quite white. I must be careful not to play any more tricks on her.

Lizzie sat down in her sitting-room and slowly unfastened her bonnet and lifted it from her bright hair. It must have been a trick of her imagination. Now she felt nothing. The fright Gerald had given her at the lake must have over-set her.

There was a scratching at the door and she called, 'Come in.'

The door opened and Peter Bond walked into the room.

'Peter,' said Lizzie. 'Do sit down and chat to me. How is your fair Sarah?'

'I am at my wit's end,' said Peter with a groan.

'Why, has she snubbed you?'

'Not at all, Lizzie, she is all that is amiable. But I had forgotten that Sarah is very dreamy. Although we talked of people we know in our village, it was as if most of her mind was somewhere else.'

'Sarah Walters *is* very dreamy,' said Lizzie. 'Are you sure ... I do not wish to offend you ... but are you sure you would wish to be allied to such a family? Squire Walters seems a terrible old man and his poor wife appears to be frightened to open her mouth.'

Peter clasped his hands and stared at Lizzie beseechingly. 'I am sure she would be glad to escape from her family.'

'How can I say this?' Lizzie looked at him sadly.

'Such an invitation to such a family from the great Duke of Severnshire must have given them hopes of a marriage for Sarah, and not with you either.'

'They must see that such a match is unthinkable.'

'And yet what else can they think?' said Lizzie patiently. 'The Walters are not in the way of receiving invitations from dukes.'

'But they must know it was because of me!'

'The squire has great vanity, I think,' said Lizzie. 'And Sarah did not recognize you. Was she even aware of your existence?'

'We danced several times at the local assemblies, and then, one beautiful day which will live in my memory forever, I was out walking and I met her. We walked and talked for an hour.'

'And did Sarah show any warmth towards you?'

'Oh, yes, she said I was the easiest person to talk to she had ever met.'

'And what did you talk about?' asked Lizzie curiously.

It transpired that Peter had done most of the talking. The local vicar had introduced Peter to his bishop and the bishop had given Peter a letter of introduction to the duke. Peter had talked of his hopes of securing a position as secretary in the duke's household.

'I will try to become friendly with Sarah,' said Lizzie at last, 'and try to find out if she has any feelings for you.'

'Would you? You are the best of friends. Tell me, do you approve of my choice of beau for you?'

'Mr Parkes is very handsome,' said Lizzie

71

cautiously. 'He appears sunny and good-natured. Farther than that, I have no opinion.'

When Peter had left, Lizzie went next door to talk to Miss Trumble.

She wondered whether to tell Miss Trumble about her odd feeling that the house was angry with her, but decided against it. Miss Trumble would worry that the old Beverley obsession with Mannerling had returned.

Instead she told Miss Trumble about Peter's worries. 'There is not much hope there,' said Miss Trumble, 'unless the obvious hopes of the squire are well and truly dashed and the duke says something about allowing Mr Bond to marry and set up his establishment.'

'Could you speak to him about it?' pleaded Lizzie.

'Gervase is ... difficult. He is still angry with me for remaining at my post. But we will see. How did you find Mr Parkes?'

'Very handsome. Very cheerful.'

'Try to look beyond his looks, Lizzie. I sense a carelessness and heedlessness there.'

'He is very young,' said Lizzie sententiously.

Miss Trumble smiled. 'And you so old. Now let us repair to your rooms and get you ready for dinner. The duke keeps fashionably late hours. Seven-thirty for dinner! I remember when not so long ago dinner was served at four in the after-noon.'

The duke, without thinking, took his aunt in to dinner, as she was the highest-ranking lady there. Lady Verity frowned awfully and Celia flounced.

Sarah was, in her head, setting up her nursery, having successfully married the duke. Squire Walters greedily surveyed the table. Such a profligacy of dishes! This could be the sort of life the Walters family could lead if only his daughter would make a push to attract the duke.

Lizzie was placed between Gerald and Peter. The secretary's presence at the dinner-table made the Earl and Countess of Hernshire think their host must be an eccentric. Sarah was on Peter's other side, but to his despair she answered all his sallies with monosyllabic answers. He did not know that he was interrupting a really splendid dream.

When the ladies retired to the drawing-room, to leave the gentlemen to their wine, Lizzie went to sit beside Sarah. 'You must be delighted to meet Mr Bond again,' she began.

'Mr–'

'Bond,' said Lizzie sharply. 'The duke's secretary.'

'Ah, yes,' said Sarah. 'Mr Bond is very kind, I think.'

'Do you know why you and your parents were invited?' demanded Lizzie.

Sarah blushed slightly and looked down at her hands. 'Why, Papa says he must have heard of me and considered me a suitable lady to make his bride.'

'That was not the case at all,' said Lizzie. 'It was Peter, Mr Bond, who prompted the duke into asking you.'

Sarah looked at her in bewilderment and then her face cleared. 'That explains how His Grace came to learn of me.'

'Yes.'

'He must have asked Mr Bond to find him a suitable lady,' said Sarah with a little laugh, 'and Mr Bond remembered me. How clever of him!'

Lizzie raised her eyes to the painted ceiling in exasperation. 'My dear widgeon, Mr Bond has formed a tendre for you and his sympathetic master, on learning of it, suggested he invite you and your parents.'

Now she had Sarah's full and undivided attention as all her rosy dreams of marriage and children and being a duchess whirled about her head and disappeared. She raised her hands to her white face. 'That cannot be true. It *must* not be true!'

'Mr Bond is a friend of mine and an excellent gentleman.'

'But he is only a secretary!'

'And you are only a squire's daughter,' said Lizzie brutally.

Sarah eyes swam with tears. 'Papa will be furious. He will say it is all my fault and he will shout at me and call me useless.'

'There now,' said Lizzie, pressing the girl's cold hand. 'We will think of something.'

In the dining-room, the duke stifled a yawn. The various fathers were pressing on him descriptions of the beauty and wit of their daughters. It was all quite vulgar and he had only himself to blame for having behaved vulgarly, for having gone shopping for a bride, as if he had sent for lengths of cloth on approval. But one did not need to entertain lengths of cloth or entertain the shopkeeper's family.

He had a sudden bright picture in his head of Lizzie and young Gerald. Had he, Gervase, tenth Duke of Severnshire, ever laughed in the sunlight with a young lady? Not that he could remember. The sad fact was one could not choose a bride in the way one chose a mistress. If he married some lady, she would bear his children and be part of his life. There was Lady Verity, of impeccable lineage and impeccable hauteur. Were he to marry her, they would settle down to a correct life with children relegated to the nursery and produced occasionally before dinner for his inspection. She would never play with them or worry about them. And yet what was so strange about that? It was the way of the world. But she would not be popular with his tenants and servants, a fact he had not hitherto considered important. As for Celia Charters, he would strangle her one day at the breakfast table, being unable to take her mindless prattle any longer. He was alarmed that the dreadful squire with the crushed wife appeared to assume that Sarah had been selected as a possible candidate.

He began to wonder how soon he could be shot of the lot of them and what excuse he could make to get rid of them. Perhaps Mr Bond could think of something. His thoughts turned to his excellent secretary. Come to think of it, he saw no reason why Mr Bond should not marry. He could live in a house on the estate and report each day for his duties.

He cut the conversation short by rising to his

feet. 'Shall we join the ladies?'

He noticed the way Gerald crossed immediately to Lizzie's side. Lizzie was sitting with Sarah Walters. Mr Bond joined them and the four were soon chatting happily, or so it looked to him.

He had a sudden desire that little Lizzie Beverley would notice him. He crossed to join them and all conversation died.

'Miss Beverley,' he said, 'I crave a few moments of your attention.'

Lizzie rose reluctantly and curtsied. He led her to a corner of the room.

'Yes, Your Grace?'

'I am interested to find out how Mr Bond is faring with Miss Walters.'

'Alas,' said Lizzie, 'Miss Walters was under the impression that she had been invited as a suitable bride for you. I disabused her. But whether she will notice Mr Bond is in question. Love is a strange thing. You cannot choose whom you will love. You cannot make yourself love someone just because they are suitable, or so my sisters tell me.'

'I think love is an invention of poets and balladmongers,' he said harshly.

'I suppose you would,' said Lizzie candidly, 'never having had the need of anyone or any affection.'

'But you are different?'

'I think I would rather be like Miss Trumble than be married to someone whom I did not love or respect. I am very fortunate. With all my sisters married so well, I do not *have* to marry.'

'I would have thought the alternative would

76

have distressed you. Confined to the country with nothing much to occupy your time.'

'As to that, I can visit my sisters, and be a good aunt to their children. I have my books for company and my dreams.'

'And what do you dream of?'

'Other countries. I would like to see some of the places I have only read about in books.'

'Do you ride?'

'I used to ride when we lived here. But at home, we have only the carriage horse.'

'Perhaps you might care to ride out with me tomorrow?'

'But you will be neglecting your guests!'

'I doubt if any of them will rise before noon. Do you rise early?'

'Yes, Your Grace.'

'Then I will meet you in the hall at nine – provided the weather stays fine.'

'Thank you,' said Lizzie demurely. Her eyes strayed to Gerald, who was now talking to Celia and looking very well amused.

Sarah was only lending half an ear to Mr Bond's conversation. She watched Lizzie and the duke. What was Lizzie saying? Sarah longed for her dream about the duke to come back. The world was such a drab place without dreams and her wedding to the duke had been a simply splendid one.

When she saw Lizzie coming back, Sarah rose and went to join her, leaving Peter with a sentence unfinished.

'What were you talking about?' asked Sarah eagerly. 'Did he mention me?'

'He was anxious to know how Mr Bond's suit was faring.'

Sarah's face fell. 'And for some odd reason,' said Lizzie, 'he wishes me to go riding with him tomorrow.'

'But you are not even a candidate for marriage!' exclaimed Sarah, biting her lip. 'Why should he waste time with you?'

'I suppose it is some sort of whim,' said Lizzie. 'I am to meet him in the hall at nine o'clock. Shall we join Mr Bond and Mr Parkes?'

Sarah went back and resumed her seat next to Mr Bond, but her eyes were fixed on the middle distance. And then she thought she saw it all. Lizzie Beverley wanted the duke for herself. Had not her own father warned her just before dinner that he had learned from their maid of the legendary Beverley obsession to regain Mannerling through marriage? Her face cleared. Lizzie must have invented that story about Mr Bond. She felt all at once very courageous and scheming. Lizzie would not be there at nine o'clock, but *she* would. Her eyes clouded up with happy dreams as she rode out across the sunny countryside on a milk-white steed at the side of the duke.

It was only when the company retired for the night that Sarah came out of her dreams and into the reality of the fact that she had nothing planned to stop Lizzie Beverley from going on that ride.

Her maid brought her in her usual glass of hot milk on a tray. When the maid had retired, Sarah slowly went over to the toilet-table and picked up a bottle of laudanum. She tipped the contents into the glass of milk, and then rang the bell.

When a footman answered it, Sarah said, 'Pray take this milk to Miss Lizzie Beverley. It was given to me by mistake.'

The footman bowed, picked up the tray and left.

He carried it along the corridor to the west wing and scratched at Lizzie's door, and then hearing a faint 'Come in,' opened it and carried the milk over to Lizzie, who was in bed, and placed it on the table beside her.

'What is this?' asked Lizzie sleepily.

'It is hot milk, miss.'

'I did not ask for any.'

'Miss Walters sent it to you. She said it had been given to her by mistake.'

'It is not for me. Ugh, it is getting cold already. Leave it.'

When the footman had left, Lizzie turned on her side and went to sleep, leaving the milk untouched.

Sarah awoke very early. She had already laid out her riding-dress. What if Lizzie had not drunk the milk?

She impatiently rang the bell. Sarah felt slightly guilty at sending for a servant so early but then decided that as a future duchess, she must learn to be authoritative. A sleepy footman finally answered, and to her question said that Miss Beverley was in the Blue Room in the west wing. Sarah waited a few moments after he had left and then hurriedly dressed and made her way along the corridors to the west wing. She stood outside the Blue Room and then gently turned the handle of the door and opened it. She found herself in Lizzie's sitting-room. The key was on the inside of the sitting-room door. Sarah locked it and put the key in her pocket. Then she crept through the door which connected the sitting-room to the bedroom. Lizzie had woken during the night and knocked over the glass of milk with her elbow. She had sponged up the fallen liquid and replaced the glass and gone back to sleep. Sarah saw the empty glass and Lizzie apparently in a drugged sleep. But just to make doubly sure...

She extracted the key from the inside of the bedroom door, went out and locked the door behind her. There now, she thought. I am become a veritable Lady Macbeth! Now all I have to do is wait until nine o'clock.

FOUR

It is impossible, in our condition of Society, not to be sometimes a Snob.
WILLIAM MAKEPEACE THACKERAY

Lizzie did not have a lady's-maid, since Betty, who acted as such to the Beverleys, had gone to Bath with her mother. She did not want to rouse Miss Trumble, for that lady might protest at her going out unchaperoned.

So she dressed herself in a smart riding outfit of dark-green velvet and put a saucy little green velvet top hat on her head, angling it rakishly to the side to show off her glossy curls.

Lizzie glanced at the clock. Five to nine. She went to her bedroom door and found it locked. Irritated, she went through to her sitting-room and found that door locked as well.

She rang the bell, and waited and waited while the clock began to chime out nine silvery strokes.

Wondering why no one was answering the bell, she opened the window and looked out. The west wing curved round and so she had a perfect picture of the duke, two horses, one groom – and Sarah Walters standing outside the house.

Lizzie stared. Sarah was in riding-dress. Her own doors were locked and no one came. And then there was that glass of milk. Her green eyes hardened. A stout creeper grew outside the window. Lizzie hitched up her riding-dress and climbed over the sill.

'It is very kind of you to offer yourself as a riding companion,' the duke was saying frostily to Sarah. 'But I am sure Miss Beverley will be here directly.'

'I am always punctual,' said Sarah, 'and cannot quite understand anyone who is not.'

Sarah was supremely confident that Lizzie would not appear. She, Sarah Walters, had thought of everything. If the laudanum had not worked, then the doors were locked, and if Lizzie rang the bell, then no one would answer it, for Sarah had remembered at the last minute that, of course, she would ring, and so had been lucky in finding the servants' hall empty, as all were about their duties,

81

and had cut the bell-wire which led to Lizzie's room.

The duke had been brought up to be supremely aware of his great position in the social scale. Lizzie should not find him waiting. On the other hand, he had no intention of encouraging the pretentions of Sarah Walters, and he also found it highly suspicious that she should be so conveniently on hand and at the right time attired in riding-dress.

'I have decided that I will keep to my own company, Miss Walters,' he said. 'Good day to you.'

'Oh, I see I will have to tell you the truth,' said Sarah, thinking quickly. 'Lizzie Beverley sent me in her stead.'

'Why? Is she ill?'

'No, she said she could not be troubled. She would rather go riding later with Mr Parkes.'

'Be damned to her,' muttered the duke. He turned to glare at the west wing and then froze. A slight figure in green velvet was climbing nimbly down a creeper.

He gave an exclamation and sprang onto his horse and rode until he was under that descending figure.

'What are you about, Miss Beverley?' he called up to her.

She twisted round and shouted down to him. 'Someone locked me in my room.'

He dismounted and held up his arms. 'I seem destined to lift you down out of shrubbery.'

Sarah saw Lizzie tumbling down into the duke's waiting arms and with a little gasp of fright ran back into the house. She replaced the keys in the

82

doors of Lizzie's bedroom and sitting-room. Shaking with fright, she wondered what to do about the cut bell-wire. But there was nothing she could do about it. She went to her own room and sat there, trembling and biting her nails.

'I find it most odd,' said the duke, 'that you should be locked in your room, that your bell does not work, and that Miss Walters should tell me that you had told her to go in your stead. I think we should both go in and confront her and then I will send her packing.'

Lizzie felt all her fury at Sarah ebbing away. Peter must find out for himself how awful she was. Poor Peter. And he would be heartbroken were Sarah to be sent away in disgrace.

'I think you must forgive her,' said Lizzie. 'Miss Walters is under great pressure from her father, I think. You see, the Walters family do not know that the invitation really came from Mr Bond. They think that for some reason you have decided to look their daughter over as a possible candidate to become duchess.'

'No one can be so vain or so stupid!'

'When it comes to the prospect of having a daughter who might become a duchess, most of the world can turn vain and stupid. I did tell Miss Walters that her invitation was due entirely to Mr Bond, but perhaps she did not believe me.'

'But if your bell did not ring in the servants' hall because she had cut the wire, then I cannot let it go past without saying something. Wait here. I shall not be long.'

The duke went to the servants' hall and looked

at the cut wire. Then he went straight up to Sarah's room and opened her sitting-room door. Sarah was crouched in a chair by the window, her eyes red with weeping.

She gasped when she saw him and struggled to her feet.

'You have behaved disgracefully,' said the duke. 'You locked Miss Beverley in her rooms, you cut the bell-wire, and you lied to me. I have a good mind to send you packing, although for some charitable reason, Miss Beverley has begged me not to.'

Sarah fell to her knees and raised her clasped hands to him. 'I beg you, Your Grace,' she said in a choked voice, 'do not send me away. My father will beat me.'

Squire Walters, for all his parsimony and verbal bullying, had never struck his daughter. He sometimes hit his wife when he had drunk too much, but so far had not laid a hand on his daughter.

The duke suddenly felt a great weariness and distaste. 'I believe Miss Beverley told you that you had been invited here solely because of Mr Bond. It is an invitation that I regret.' Great tears rolled down Sarah's wan cheeks.

'There, now,' said the duke, relenting. 'Your father will not get to hear of this and you may stay. But there must be no repetition of your behaviour this morning.'

Sarah seized his hand and kissed it.

'Please rise, Miss Walters. Such behaviour is undignified and does you no credit. I am not the Pope.'

Sarah got to her feet and stood before him, the

picture of misery.

He patted her on the head. 'You silly girl,' he said gently. 'We will say no more about it.'

He strode from the room. Sarah sat down shakily. He had taken pity on her. He had patted her hair! They had had their first row. How they would look back on it and laugh! Dreams flooded her brain, which only a few minutes ago had been black with misery.

'I am beginning to wonder if Miss Walters is quite sane,' said the duke when he rejoined Lizzie.

But Lizzie was determined to be loyal to Mr Bond and try to support this odd object of his love. 'I think her parents' ambitions temporarily overset her mind,' she said. 'She appears quite a gentle, dreamy creature.'

'I think she has wasted enough of the day. Shall we be on our way, Miss Beverley?'

Lady Verity stood by the window of her bedroom, stretching and yawning. And then she saw the duke and Lizzie riding off down the drive.

She had not considered Lizzie any competition at all. Such an odd little girl. What was going on?

Her usually doting father had alarmed her the evening before by calling on her before she went to sleep. 'Severnshire don't seem interested in you, Verity,' he said bluntly. 'You ain't going to secure a duke, so if you take my advice, you'll come down off your high horse and take the next offer you get, or you'll end up an ape-leader.'

For the very first time it began to dawn on Verity that she might be left on the shelf. The invitation to the duke's had meant to her that she had been right in refusing previous offers and so saving herself for the prize. That this prize might be snatched away from her by a redhead barely out of the schoolroom was past bearing. She needed an ally. Celia was her rival. But Celia might be of help in blocking the pretentions of this Beverley.

She rang for her maid and stood impatiently while she was dressed. Then she went to Celia's room and walked in. Celia was fast asleep. Verity shook her awake.

'What is it?' demanded Celia sleepily. 'Oh, it's you.'

Verity sat on the end of Celia's bed. 'Something has to be done about Lizzie Beverley,' she began.

'Who? What?'

'Oh, do wake up,' said Verity crossly. 'I never thought of Lizzie as a rival. But she has gone off riding with the duke.'

Celia struggled up against the pillows. 'Well, she's local. Gone to see a sick tenant or something.'

Verity got up and began to pace up and down the room. 'I think there is more to it than that. Do you remember all the gossip about the Beverleys? How they plotted and schemed to get Mannerling back? And the duke watched her a lot last night, and then he drew her aside and began to talk to her. I think we have a serious rival there.'

'But what can we do?' asked Celia, fully awake now. 'And we cannot both marry him.'

'Agreed, but unless we get Lizzie out of the field, then neither of us is going to marry him.

86

Let's deal with her first and then let the best lady win!'

'But how?'

'We must think of something.'

After an energetic gallop, the duke slowed his mount and finally stopped on a rise overlooking the market town of Hedgefield. 'You are a good rider,' he said to Lizzie.

'It is a good horse,' said Lizzie, patting the animal's neck. 'The countryside looks beautiful today.'

Small neat fields lay spread out before them in the warm sun. A dog barked nearby and a flock of rooks wheeled up to the blue sky.

Lizzie looked at him curiously. His face was handsome but there was a hardness about the mouth and his hooded eyes, and yet it was not a cruel face.

'Why do you look at me so, miss?'

'I was wondering why you had never married.'

His silvery eyes glinted with sudden amusement. 'Do you want to marry me, Miss Lizzie?'

'No, I do not think that would be a very good idea.'

'Why?'

'You are too ... hard. Uncompromising. I feel that a wife to you would be another sort of servant, expected to do her job impeccably in return for your title and fortune. I do not think you would expect her either to argue with you or disapprove of you in any way. In fact, you would probably be shocked if she did so.'

'What makes you think you know me so well

after such a short acquaintanceship?'

'I can recognize pride,' said Lizzie with a little sigh. 'And who better than I to do so. The Beverleys were famous for their hauteur.'

'You are wrong in your assessment of my character. I do not cut worthy people, only pretentious people.'

'It is just that I think you do not really notice other people's feelings.'

'And why should I? I do not ill-treat anyone.'

'But perhaps you might have to consider another person's feelings were you to marry.'

'You are romantical. When in this day and age does a husband worry his head about his wife's maundering sensibilities? A good wife obeys her husband and sees that his establishment is well-run.'

'What of happiness?'

'Happiness? There is enjoyment in good books, good exercise, and in good heart.'

'If I were to marry for that kind of happiness, I would be less than my sisters.'

'You are young, Miss Lizzie. You will grow out of such longings and fantasies.'

'But you did not have to.'

'I do not understand you,' said the duke.

'I mean,' said Lizzie patiently, 'that having never been plagued with either longings or fantasies in your youth, you had nothing to grow out of.'

'Pert, but true.' Then that mirror image flashed before the duke's eyes, that terrible old man, and he shifted uneasily in the saddle.

'How do you see me when I become really old?' he asked.

Lizzie tilted her head on one side and surveyed him curiously. 'Very stately, still upright, grim-faced, autocratic. The glimmer of kindness which inspired you to invite Sarah for Peter will not return.'

'Peter? You mean Mr Bond?'

'Yes, he is my friend, so I call him Peter, but not in company.'

'So you consider me unkind?'

'Unthinking.'

'You do not have a very high opinion of my character, Miss Lizzie.'

'I am being very rude,' said Lizzie contritely. 'I do apologize.'

'You possibly do not understand me because of the difference in our ages,' he said stiffly.

'I do not think that is the case. Your aunt is very old and yet she has a youthful spirit. I converse with her on easy terms.'

'So you find me uncomfortable company?'

'A trifle intimidating, Your Grace, that I do admit.'

He smiled down at her, the rather harsh lines of his face softening, and she felt a treacherous tug at her heart. 'Where shall we go now?' he asked.

'What is your pleasure?'

'I am thirsty. My pleasure is a long, cold drink.'

'Then we will ride to the Green Man in Hedge-field,' said Lizzie. 'Normally it would not be quite correct for me to be seen in the taproom, but we could sit at a table outside in the sun.'

He nodded and spurred his horse and Lizzie flew after him, watching his tall figure and wondering why he did not tire of her company, especially after all the rude things she had said about him.

At that very moment, Peter was in a quandary. He was walking in the gardens with Sarah and listening in increasing dismay to her tale about how the duke had formed a tendre for her. She told him that she had been frightened that Lizzie would engage the duke's affections and so she had tried to go in her stead.

'My dear Miss Walters!' exclaimed Peter when she had finished, 'I beg of you to be sensible. A whole bottle of laudanum might have killed Miss Beverley. Have you thought of that? It is a miracle my master did not send you away. Miss Beverley told nothing but the truth. It was because of me that you were invited.'

She turned glowing eyes to his worried face. 'Ah, yes, I understand that now. But if you could have seen the gentle way he patted my head.'

'Miss Walters, I beg of you to stop this folly. His Grace would never propose to you.'

'You are jealous!'

'I am distressed.'

I think you are mad, he thought bleakly. I must warn my master. What have I done?

'Excuse me,' he said abruptly. 'I have business to attend to.'

But he went into the house and changed into his riding clothes. He was very much shaken. His darling Sarah had turned into an unstable monster. His master had gone out riding. He could not wait. He must warn him.

Farmer Moon's daughter, Tiffin, was jolting along in a post-chaise by the walls of the Mannerling estate next to her acidulous aunt, Bertha, and wishing she were dead. Like many wealthy farmers, Jack Moon aspired to the ways and manners of the gentry. His wife had died some years ago, a sensible woman, and so there was no one to curb his ambition. He had sent Tiffany, nicknamed Tiffin, a sweet-faced girl with wide brown eyes and brown curly hair, to a seminary for young ladies in Bath. Tiffin's schooldays were now over. Her grim aunt had been sent to escort her home. Already she missed the friends she had made at the seminary, but knew that because of their higher social position she would never see them again.

Although she told herself firmly that she should not expect God to intercede in the petty little life of one Tiffany Moon, she could not help praying that something would happen to alter her state so that she would not need to be condemned to a life of embarrassment while her father sought a suitor for her amongst the ranks of his betters and watch him getting well and truly snubbed for his pains.

It was just then that the pole of the post-chaise broke, right outside the tall iron gates of Mannerling. Aunt Bertha catapulted across the tiny carriage and banged her head. Tiffin was tumbled onto the floor. She wrenched open the door and got down on the road. The driver had got down as well and was holding on to the reins of the plunging horse.

Tiffin looked desperately back into the carriage at her aunt, who was lying crumpled and still on

91

the floor.

'Help!' she cried. 'My aunt. Something awful has happened.'

And that was when Peter came riding up to the gates. The lodge-keeper came out to open them, saw the post-chaise lurched on one side and the distressed Tiffin and called to Peter, 'Accident, sir.'

He swung the gates open. Peter dismounted and ran to Tiffin.

'It is my aunt, sir,' she said. 'Oh, let her not be dead.'

Peter wrenched open the other door of the carriage. He gently felt Aunt Bertha's pulse.

'I think she is unconscious, miss,' said Peter. The driver joined them. 'Wait here and I will ride to the house for help.'

'Oh, thank you, sir,' said Tiffin, her large eyes swimming with tears.

She sat on the carriage step holding her aunt's hand and feeling wicked – oh, so wicked. This is what came of her prayers. Poor Aunt, thought soft-hearted Tiffin, forgetting how much she detested the woman.

Peter returned with a carriage and servants. Aunt Bertha was lifted tenderly into the carriage. 'If you will join her, Miss...?'

'Moon. Miss Moon,' said Tiffin.

'Please do not look so alarmed, Miss Moon,' said Peter gently. 'A footman has ridden off to fetch the physician.' He climbed into the carriage with her. Tiffin took her aunt's head on her lap and Peter sat opposite. 'Are people waiting for you?' he asked. 'What is your direction?'

'Moon's Farm, about twenty miles from the border of your estates, Your Grace.'

'I am only the duke's secretary,' said Peter. 'My name is Bond. Please do not look so distressed.'

'I thank you from the bottom of my heart,' said Tiffin.

'Think nothing of it,' said Peter, feeling very tall and gallant. There was something so fragile and appealing about the sweet face looking so trustingly up into his own. 'As soon as your aunt is settled and the physician has seen her, I will send someone to tell your parents...'

'Just my father; he is a farmer. My mother is dead.'

Tiffin gave a little gulp as the stately beauty of Mannerling hove into view, dreaming in the sunlight, the wings on either side of the house springing out in graceful curves.

But once inside, her concern was all for her aunt as she followed the servant up the stairs. Aunt Bertha was laid on a bed. The housekeeper said it would be unwise to move her further by undressing her until the physician had seen her.

The physician arrived and after examining Aunt Bertha said she had sustained a blow to the head, causing concussion. She required quiet and rest, and should not be moved for a few days.

When informed of this, Peter said to Tiffin, 'I will arrange a bedchamber for you. Your luggage from the post-chaise has already been brought to the house.'

Tiffin thanked him and then said in a miserable little voice, 'My father will no doubt arrive shortly.'

'You look so worried,' exclaimed Peter. 'He

cannot possibly blame you for an accident which was none of your doing.'

Tiffin looked at Peter's kind, sensitive face. 'I think I will tell you. May we step aside?' Her wide eyes glanced nervously at the hovering servants.

'By all means. Follow me.'

He led her a little way along the corridor and then stopped in the embrasure of a window.

'My father has great social ambitions for me,' whispered Tiffin. 'He is a good man, but arriving at a duke's house will make him...' Her voice trailed away and she turned scarlet. 'You see,' she went on after a pause, 'he sent me to a very expensive seminary in Bath. He has great hopes that I will make a grand marriage. But all the young ladies there were socially far above me, and so they are all preparing for their first Season in London next year. I have had no invitations to their homes, of course, and he will blame me for that.'

Peter felt very grand and strong and protective. 'You must not worry. I will deal with your father.'

'Oh, thank you.' How trusting those beautiful eyes were as they looked up into his own!

'Now, return to your aunt,' said Peter. 'The housekeeper will be sent to show you to your room.'

Farmer Moon read the letter from Peter describing the accident and stating that his sister would stay at Mannerling until she recovered. His heart swelled with gratitude. This Duke of Severnshire was unwed and under his roof was his pretty daughter, Tiffin.

He told the footman to wait and went into his study and brushed aside piles of farm accounts. He would not go himself. Let love blossom. Nothing must happen to remind the great duke that Tiffin was only a farmer's daughter. He laboriously penned a reply thanking this Mr Bond fulsomely for his master's hospitality to his poor daughter and his sister, Bertha. Then he sanded and sealed the badly spelled letter and took it out to the footman. When the footman rode off, he stood rubbing his hands, his head filled with as many mad dreams of glory as Sarah Walters could ever conjure up.

Lizzie was sitting in the garden of the Green Man at Hedgefield drinking lemonade with the duke.

She had given up any idea of curbing her tongue. She had also lost any fear of the duke. The inn garden was pretty, and apart from a brief wish that it were Gerald sitting opposite her instead of the duke, she felt quite at ease.

Perhaps it was because the duke seemed relaxed in her company and showed no signs of wishing to hurry back to his other guests.

She had told him frankly about the adventures of the Beverley sisters and how all had turned out well for them the minute they had decided they did not want Mannerling.

'You, at least,' said the duke, 'do not seem to be consumed with ambition to get your old home back.'

'I think there is something evil about that house,' said Lizzie. 'Do not laugh at me.'

'I have no intention of laughing at you,' he said,

remembering the face in the mirror. 'Perhaps all the intrigue and death and ambition have imprinted their mark in the walls and that creates at times a sinister atmosphere that gives us fancies. But what can a house do?'

'It calls out to people. It says, "I could be yours",' said Lizzie.

'And does it call to you?'

'You will think me mad. I do not love Mannerling any more and Mannerling is angry with me.'

'Now that *is* fancy!'

'Perhaps,' said Lizzie and buried her little nose in her lemonade glass. Then she looked up and asked candidly, 'And so, have you decided on your bride?'

He was about to reply that he had made a mistake and he could not wait for the day until he was shot of the lot of them. But there was something irksome in the very indifference of Lizzie Beverley. And yet why should she regard him as anything other than someone too old for her when she had the glorious Gerald waiting back at Mannerling for her?

So he said somewhat testily that he had not yet made up his mind.

'I think Lady Verity would suit you very well,' said Lizzie.

'Why? Why not Miss Celia Charter?'

'I consider you an intelligent man and although everyone assures me that gentlemen like stupid ladies, I have noticed that Miss Charter's prattle bores you.'

'So why Lady Verity?'

'She is rich and haughty.'

'And I am rich and haughty?'

'Well ... yes.'

'Miss Lizzie, if I were all that high in the instep, I would hardly be sitting in a common inn garden with you.'

'Nasty!' said Lizzie, her green eyes flashing.

'But oh, so true.'

'Then why are you sitting in what you call a common inn garden with such as I?'

'Because you are beautiful.'

'You are cruel,' said Lizzie angrily. 'You are mocking me!'

'Not I. Your hair gleams in the sunlight and you have a fascinating elfin charm.'

Lizzie hung her head. 'Now what have I done?' he teased. 'Nonplussed the well-educated, direct-speaking Miss Lizzie Beverley?'

'I am all that you must dislike,' said Lizzie. 'I am not stately enough. Not grand enough. Not rich enough.'

'If I had known a compliment was going to distress you so much, I would have kept silent. But did not, what I must continue to call Miss Trumble, teach you how to accept compliments?'

'Oh, yes. I must raise my fan so, and lower my eyelashes, and say, "You do flatter me", and then I should titter.'

'Now it is you who mocks me. I cannot envisage my aunt telling anyone to titter.'

'Miss Trumble has a quite wicked sense of humour. But she has great good sense and I must talk to her again about Peter.'

'My secretary?'

'Yes, Miss Walters is not for him. He is too fine

97

a gentleman to be saddled with such a mad girl.'

'You worry so much about my servant that I begin to fear you have formed a tendre for him.'

'Not I! We are friends.'

Those odd silver eyes of his suddenly looked directly into her own. 'No, it is the handsome Gerald who quickens your senses, is it not?'

'I barely know the man.'

'So you do not believe in love at first sight?'

'I know nothing of love, Your Grace. I am too young.'

'What? You who have lectured me on the existence of the beast.'

Lizzie felt suddenly tearful. She felt he was mocking her and she wished he would return to his old indifferent manner.

'You are talking *at* me,' she said crossly. 'Let us talk of something else. Why did you really buy Mannerling?'

'It seemed to me a good property, that is all. When my stay here is over, I shall lease it until such time as I want it back.'

Lizzie gave a little sigh. 'At least Mannerling to you is only a house. You do not seem to have been overcome by any strong desire to possess it.'

'No, and I am not sure I want to live there much longer,' said the duke, uneasily remembering that reflection in the mirror again. 'We have been away some time, and I am neglecting my guests. What should I do with them today?'

'We could play croquet.'

'So that you can beat me again?'

'So that your guests will have some gentle and healthy exercise.'

'Very well. Croquet it is.'

Tiffin sat by her aunt's bedside. The window was open and she could hear laughter and cries from outside as the guests played croquet. The door opened and an elderly lady came in. Tiffin rose and curtsied low.

'My name is Miss Trumble,' said the lady with a warm smile. 'I am so sorry to hear of your accident.'

'Thank you,' said Tiffin shyly.

'And let me see your poor aunt.' Miss Trumble crossed to the bed and felt Aunt Bertha's forehead. 'No fever, that is good. From my experience, she will shortly recover consciousness.' She sat down on a chair next to the bed and looked brightly at Tiffin. 'I am chaperone to a Miss Lizzie Beverley. Tell me about yourself.'

So Tiffin talked, and although she was not as frank as she had been with Peter, Miss Trumble quickly summed up the situation: ambitious farmer father, cross and bullying aunt, girl made lonely by the ambitions of her parent. Tiffin then went on to describe her rescue by Peter Bond in glowing terms.

'Yes, Mr Bond is an exceptional young man,' said Miss Trumble. 'Ah, here he is.'

'I have a letter from your father, Miss Moon,' said Peter. 'He thanks us for our hospitality but is much engaged with farm work and cannot join you.'

Relief lit up Tiffin's eyes.

'The day is too fine for you to be indoors,' said Miss Trumble. 'Mr Bond, why do you not take

Miss Moon down and introduce her to the other guests?'

Tiffin shrank back in her chair. 'Oh, I could not. I dare not.'

'Nonsense, child,' said Miss Trumble. 'Run along. I will sit with your aunt.'

Peter smiled and held out his arm.

'I am quite terrified,' whispered Tiffin as she and Peter made their way downstairs. The sheer richness of Mannerling, from painted ceilings to cornices and down to the marble tiles of the entrance hall struck fresh fear into her heart. 'Does His Grace know I am here?'

'Yes, of course. I informed him of your aunt's accident as soon as he returned.'

When they approached the party, who had just finished a game of croquet, Tiffin quailed before the battery of curious eyes. Peter led Tiffin up to the duke.

'I am pleased to make your acquaintance,' said the duke. 'You are welcome to stay until your aunt is well enough to complete her journey home.'

'Thank you,' whispered Tiffin.

'Perhaps, Mr Bond,' said the duke, 'you would be so good as to show Miss Moon the gardens? They are very fine at this time of year.'

Peter bowed and led Tiffin away. Tiffin almost skipped along beside him. As soon as they were out of earshot, she said, 'What a relief!'

'To get the introductions over with?'

'Oh, no, the duke. He is so old!'

'He is thirty-four, Miss Moon.'

'Yes, but that is old indeed, so neither Aunt nor Papa can entertain any ambitions there.'

'I would be surprised if they entertained any ambitions at all,' said Peter drily.

'You do not know them. When it comes to social ambition, I think people go a little mad.'

'You have the right of it,' said Peter gloomily. The duke on his return had given his secretary a brief and pithy account of Miss Walters's disgraceful behaviour and Peter had not been able to find the courage to tell his master that Sarah was unrepentant. As they turned into the rose garden, Peter had a desire to confide in someone. He had been hoping to have a private word with Lizzie, but that might not be until the evening, and the desire to unburden himself was great. He found himself telling Tiffin all about Sarah Walters.

'Really. How terrible!' exclaimed Tiffin. 'If she cannot appreciate you for the fine and brave man you are and worth a hundred dukes, she is not worth knowing!'

And although Peter smiled sadly, the large eyes turned up to his own warmed his heart.

'What a little charmer,' said Gerald after Tiffin was led away. 'Such eyes!'

Lizzie felt cast down. The duke was walking a little way away with Lady Verity. She had to admit to herself ruefully that she had had a little hope that Gerald might turn out to be the amiable husband that she sometimes longed for.

'Who was that odd creature?' Lady Verity was asking the duke.

'If you mean the pretty and charming Miss Moon,' said the duke, 'the pole of her carriage broke outside the gates and her aunt was knocked unconscious. Miss Moon will be staying until her aunt is recovered.'

'How very convenient that her carriage broke down where it did,' said Lady Verity acidly. 'A farmer's daughter, too! But I, too, am used to the machinations of pretentious people.'

'Miss Moon appears sweet and innocent,' he said coldly. What had Gerald Parkes said to take the sunshine from Lizzie's face?

Sarah Walters looked moodily off in the direction that Peter had gone. She had decided to use Mr Bond for her own ends. He must know his master better than anyone and she planned to pump him for information.

Her father, who had been sitting with his wife on a chair on the lawn, rose and headed in her direction. The duke, Sarah noticed, had left Lady Verity and was heading towards Lizzie. She moved quickly to his side and said, 'I beg you to forgive me.'

'I already have,' he said crossly. Lizzie was moving off with Gerald. Where were they going?

Sarah put a confiding hand on his arm. 'Thank you,' she breathed.

Only politeness restrained the duke from shaking off that hand. The squire gave himself a gleeful little hug and returned to his chair. Little Sarah was doing very well.

When Gerald and Lizzie walked into the rose garden, Peter found he was quite annoyed to have his conversation with Tiffin disturbed, particularly when Gerald swept forward and began to ask Tiffin about her aunt and then took her arm and began to lead her off down the path amongst the rose bushes, leaving him with Lizzie.

'Oh dear, Peter,' said Lizzie. 'I do not think we should leave them alone.'

'Why?'

'I fear Mr Parkes is restless and bored and perhaps he means to enliven his stay in the country by flirting with that innocent.'

'Then let us follow them,' said Peter eagerly.

A footman came up. 'Mr Bond, His Grace requires your presence in the study.'

'Go along, Mr Bond,' urged Lizzie, formal in the presence of the servant. 'I will attend to matters.'

'Lizzie?'

Lizzie turned and saw Miss Trumble coming towards her. 'Where were you this morning?' asked Miss Trumble. 'I was looking for you. The physician is with Miss Moon's aunt and so I have a temporary respite. I promised Miss Moon I would look after her aunt while she joined the rest of you in the sunshine. Where is she? She is not with the rest.'

'She is here in the rose garden with Mr Parkes. I went out riding this morning with the duke. We ended up in the Green Man at Hedgefield.'

'Gervase asked you to go riding with him?'

'Yes, Miss Trumble. But to more important matters. Miss Moon is very sweet and innocent and I fear the wretched Gerald is planning some sort of dalliance. Do come along with me and spike his guns.'

'By all means. Our little Tiffin – ridiculous name – seemed quite taken by Mr Bond.'

'Oh, but she is, and she is just the sort of lady to turn his mind from the dreadful Sarah.'

Quickly Lizzie told Miss Trumble about Sarah's iniquities.

Miss Trumble gave a little shiver and said half to herself, 'It is quite amazing how Mannerling appears to warp minds. Ah, there is our quarry.'

Gerald was standing by a sundial. He was holding Tiffin's hand in his own and she was blushing with confusion.

'Miss Moon,' said Miss Trumble, 'the physician is attending your aunt. If you return with me, we will find out his verdict on her condition.'

Lizzie noticed that Tiffin seemed pleased to have an excuse to escape from Gerald.

'I was doing very well,' said Gerald crossly, looking after Tiffin and Miss Trumble.

'I do not want you to do very well,' said Lizzie.

'Jealous?'

'You flatter yourself, sir. That is one very vulnerable and innocent lady, and unless you mean marriage, you have no right to pursue her.'

He tucked her hand in his arm and led her back out of the rose garden. 'I would never have taken you for a moralist, Miss Lizzie.'

'I am kind and you are not.'

'You are too severe. All ladies enjoy dalliance.'

'Miss Moon has a socially ambitious father. Dally much more and you will find yourself at the altar with a shotgun in your back.'

'You dare to challenge me? You have just added the necessary spice of danger to a boring visit. I shall continue to pursue Miss Moon.'

'And I shall do everything to stop you!'

He flung a careless arm about her shoulders and gave her a hug. 'You *are* jealous!'

The duke, emerging from the house with Peter, saw that hug and his face darkened. There was something about Gerald's glowing good looks and youth which kept reminding him of that dreadful reflection in the mirror of himself as a twisted old man.

Lizzie disengaged herself from Gerald and ran forward. 'Mr Bond, if His Grace can spare you for a few moments...'

'Certainly,' said the duke sourly, thinking Lizzie was a trifle too forward in befriending gentlemen. He would need to speak to his aunt about it.

Lizzie walked a little way away with Peter. 'Peter, do you like Miss Moon?'

'I do not know her very well, but she seems a charming young lady.'

'A young lady in need of rescuing!'

'From what or whom?'

'From Mr Gerald Parkes. He is chasing her and he does not have marriage in mind.'

'What can I do?'

'Oh, she does admire you so, Peter. Do try to cut Gerald out.'

'How can I do that? I am only the duke's secretary. Besides, what of Miss Walters?'

'You cannot have the slightest feeling left for Miss Walters after the way she has behaved!'

'I am shocked by her,' said Peter slowly, 'but one must make allowances...'

'For what? For mad, murderous behaviour?'

'You are too harsh.'

Lizzie stamped her foot. 'Men! I despair for the lot of you. I shall warn Miss Moon about Gerald myself!'

Later that day the duke was dressed to go out riding to see a tenant farmer. He reached the first landing overlooking the Great Hall and found Miss Trumble looking at the great chandelier, which was on eye-level with the landing. 'It was from that chandelier that Judd hanged himself,' said Miss Trumble.

'A pox on Judd,' he said testily. 'I would speak with you about the behaviour of your charge. She is much too free and easy in her manner towards the gentlemen. You should curb her.'

'As to that, Gervase, I must ask you your intentions towards Lizzie Beverley.'

'I beg your pardon, Aunt!'

'Everyone here knows you are looking for a bride and yet you go out riding alone with Lizzie without even asking my permission to do so. You are seen with her in a common inn in Hedgefield. I ask you again. What are your intentions?'

'I do not have any *intentions* towards Lizzie Beverley,' he said wrathfully. 'She is at times an amusing chit, that is all. If you think I could possibly be considering allying my great name with a pert miss barely out of the schoolroom, you must be mad. I have no intention of marrying Lizzie Beverley. Good day to you, Aunt!'

He strode down the stairs and stood under the chandelier in the centre of the hall, drawing on his gloves.

Lizzie entered through the open main door and stood looking at him, her hand to her mouth. For suddenly the atmosphere of hate and menace emanating from the very walls of

Mannerling was terrifying.

Afterwards, she did not know what possessed her. She suddenly flew across the hall and cannoned into him. Tall and strong as he was, the duke was taken by surprise, stumbled backwards across the hall and fell headlong, with Lizzie on top of him.

The great chandelier came crashing down right onto the spot where he had been standing a moment before. Lizzie buried her head in his chest as shards of crystal flew about the hall.

There was a stunned silence and then the sound of running feet.

Lizzie began to cry with fright, hot tears soaking into the duke's cravat.

He struggled upright, still holding her. 'How did you know?' he asked.

Lizzie brushed away her tears from her white face. 'There was a sudden feeling of hate. I acted instinctively.'

'You saved my life,' he said through dry lips. The wreck of the chandelier was lit from above by a shaft of sunlight striking through the glass of the cupola at the top of the stairs. The crystals winked at them like so many glittering little elfin eyes.

'Sell this place! Leave here, Gervase!' Miss Trumble shouted from the landing.

The servants agreed afterwards that the Beverley girl's governess must have indeed been out of her wits with fright to address their master by his first name.

'We cannot let this go unchecked,' said Lady

Verity. She was being dressed for dinner by her maid while Celia sat in a chair in Verity's room.

'She saved his life,' said Celia gloomily. 'How can we rival that?'

'Lizzie Beverley appears quite taken with Mr Parkes.'

'Mr Parkes shows no interest now in anyone other than that vulgar little farmer's daughter and her simpering ways.'

'Wait for a moment. I am thinking very hard.' Verity held up a hand. 'We have been despising Lizzie, but there is something in her character which obviously attracts the duke. There is a certain wildness in her and lack of discretion.'

Celia brightened. She thought her own girlish manner was closer to that of Lizzie's than the cold Verity.

'So you think we should emulate her behaviour?' she asked.

'I think we should befriend her, find out all about her. Know thine enemy.'

'I cannot understand why that odd governess of hers is held in such high regard,' said Celia.

'As to that, I think she is probably related to the duke on the wrong side of the blanket, some mistake of his late father,' said Verity with a worldly-wise air. 'But I will not stoop to befriending a servant, particularly one who puts herself forward.'

'Perhaps you had better leave Lizzie to me,' said Celia. 'I have a more open and confiding manner than you, Verity.'

'But you do not have either my acumen or intelligence,' said Verity dismissively, and for one little moment Celia actually wished Lizzie Beverley well and hoped that she *would* secure the duke if only to bring down this haughty miss a peg.

Not far away Miss Trumble was interrogating Lizzie about her ride with the duke. 'Gentlemen are apt to amuse themselves if they can get away with it,' said Miss Trumble, 'and they are apt to forget the conventions. In future, Lizzie, if Gervase wishes to take you somewhere, then he must obtain my permission first.'

'Oh, very well,' said Lizzie.

'Having said that, I must point out you were very brave today. How did you know that chandelier was about to fall?'

Lizzie shivered. 'It was a feeling of hate from the house. I do not know how I knew the chandelier was going to fall.'

She waited for the governess to pooh-pooh this fancy, but Miss Trumble said seriously, 'Perhaps we should leave here and go home, Lizzie.'

'And leave little Miss Moon in the clutches of Gerald Parkes?'

'So Mr Parkes has fallen from grace in your eyes. Are you sure, Lizzie, you do not want him for yourself?'

'No, not at all,' said Lizzie. 'But I think I should tell Miss Moon that Gerald is only interested in dalliance.'

'That might be a good thing to do. Miss Moon is an engaging creature and much too good for such as Mr Parkes.'

'You do not like him?'

'I neither like nor dislike him. Let us just say I have met many Geralds before this.'

After Miss Trumble had left, Lizzie made her way to Tiffin's room, and finding her absent went two doors away to where she knew Aunt Bertha was to be found.

Aunt Bertha had recovered consciousness, and as Lizzie entered the room was lecturing her niece in a weak voice. 'A great opportunity has come your way,' Aunt Bertha was saying in a quavering, querulous voice. 'You must set out to win this duke. God has put you in his way, and if you do not take advantage of your situation, then God will not forgive you. Neither will I.'

Lizzie approached the bed and curtsied. 'I am glad to see you are recovered, Miss Moon.'

'Who are you?' Cold grey eyes surveyed Lizzie.

'I am Miss Beverley of Brookfield House.'

'Humph. Did I not hear the dressing-bell?'

'I will take a meal here on a tray,' said Tiffin. 'If you like, I shall read to you, Aunt.'

'Nonsense. You abuse the duke's hospitality. Go and put on your silk, the one with the bows, and mind your manners. Be off with you!'

Tiffin, as she followed Lizzie from the room, looked glad to escape. 'Will you come to my room and look at my gown?' she asked Lizzie. 'Aunt Bertha thinks it my finest but the young ladies at the seminary thought it provincial.'

'What nasty young ladies they sound!'

'Oh, no, they were only trying to be helpful.'

In Tiffin's room, Lizzie studied the gown, which was laid out on the bed. It had little bows on the shoulders and bows at the hem, and was of a depressing shade of dull pink.

'What else do you have?'

Tiffin went to the press and lifted down several gowns wrapped in tissue paper.

'Oh, this one is pretty,' said Lizzie, shaking out the folds of a blue muslin.

'Do you think so? It does not have much embellishment.'

'The colour is lovely. I will help you with your hair. Miss Trumble taught me and I am become quite clever. Sit down at the toilet-table and find me your pins.'

Tiffin obediently sat down while Lizzie began to brush out her hair.

'You must not take the attentions of Mr Parkes too seriously,' said Lizzie. 'He only plans to amuse himself.'

'I am in no danger from Mr Parkes,' said Tiffin. 'Do you know Mr Bond quite well?'

'We are friends.'

'He is a very fine man and very handsome.'

Lizzie repressed a smile. How irritated Gerald would be if he knew that Tiffin rated the secretary's sensitive and unassuming looks higher than his own.

'Yes, very handsome and very kind,' she agreed. 'But your aunt expects you to secure the duke.'

'Aunt Bertha is going to be furious with me. The duke will not even look at such as I, and he is too old.'

'Not very old,' said Lizzie. 'My sisters are all married to men older than they and are very happy.'

Tiffin studied Lizzie's reflection in the mirror. 'Do you find the duke attractive, Miss Beverley?'

'Lizzie. And I shall call you Tiffin. I find him a fine figure of a man but rather cold and autocratic.'

'Yes, he probably is,' said Tiffin. 'I only hope we may leave as soon as Aunt feels able to rise from her bed, for if she sees how indifferent the duke is to me, she will blame me for it. It is monstrous uncomfortable when one's father and aunt have social ambitions.'

'Peter will take care of you.'

'Peter?'

'Mr Bond.'

'Ah, his name is Peter. What a lovely name,' sighed Tiffin.

Lizzie suppressed a grin and began to arrange Tiffin's hair in a fashionable style.

FIVE

Intrigues half gather'd, conversation-scraps,
Kitchen-cabals, and nursery-mishaps.
GEORGE CRABBE

Perhaps Gerald would have given up any idea of pursuing Tiffin had not his parents given him a lecture before he went down to dinner. Mrs Parkes had sustained a call from Peter Bond. Peter had politely called to ask if everything was to their pleasure but had then gone on to tell Mrs

Parkes about the unexpected arrival of Miss Moon and her aunt. 'Such a charming lady,' he had said, 'but cursed with a socially ambitious father who is nothing more than a farmer and the rough type of fellow who would drive any socially presentable man who even looked at his daughter to the altar with threats of breach of promise.'

Mrs Parkes considered herself shrewd enough to recognize a warning when she heard it. She repeated to her husband what Mr Bond had said and Gerald had been summoned.

They were devoted parents but often worried about what they considered to be a wild and heedless streak in their son.

'Have you been pursuing that farmer's daughter, Miss Moon?' asked Colonel Parkes bluntly.

'Hardly,' said Gerald crossly. 'Miss Moon is just arrived and her aunt is unwell.'

'See that you don't,' said the colonel. 'Miss Moon is a respectable young lady, and unless you wish to marry her, you must treat her with respect.'

Gerald opened his blue eyes to their widest. 'I can only suppose that some jealous female has been dropping poison in your ears,' he said, thinking of Lizzie. 'I have done nothing wrong.'

'Just see that you don't,' warned the colonel.

And so when the guests gathered in the drawing-room before dinner, the very air was throbbing with schemes and plots. Verity and Celia descended on Lizzie and asked her to take a turn with them about the room. Lizzie, who knew various members of London society through her

113

sisters, chatted amiably. Her conversation was unexceptionable and both Celia and Verity were baffled. There seemed nothing particularly fascinating about Lizzie Beverley. Gerald then joined them and separated Lizzie from Celia and Verity. 'Was it necessary to warn my parents that I was chasing Miss Moon?' he demanded in an angry whisper.

'I said nothing to them,' retorted Lizzie. 'But I did drop a word of caution in Miss Moon's ear.'

'You had no right to do that,' exclaimed Gerald. 'I thought you were fun, but you have a low mind.'

'Not as low as yours,' said Lizzie sweetly.

Gerald swung away and went to join Tiffin. 'How goes your aunt?' he asked.

'Very well, I thank you,' said Tiffin.

'I find these house parties curst dull,' Gerald went on, keeping a cautious eye on his parents, who were chatting with the Chumleys. 'Do not you?'

'I have never attended a gathering like this,' said Tiffin. 'I find it all quite overwhelming. I do not know quite how to go on.'

'Tell you what,' said Gerald eagerly. 'It is a fine night. After dinner, we could go for a stroll in the gardens and I'll tell you all about things like this.'

'Would that be correct?'

'Yes, of course. I'll tell my parents, if you like.'

Tiffin hesitated and then said shyly, 'I suppose if your parents have no objection...'

Gerald crossed to his parents, bowed to the Chumleys, exchanged a few innocuous remarks about the weather, and then returned to Tiffin.

'There. That's done,' he said cheerfully. 'Conventions observed.'

Peter Bond entered. Gerald, having secured the promise of that walk, had left Tiffin. Peter bowed to the company and then joined Tiffin. 'I am so glad to see you again, Mr Bond,' confided Tiffin. 'I am not used to grand company. Although some of the young ladies at the seminary were from very grand families, I did not socialize with them, so this is different. Mr Parkes has offered to take me for a walk in the gardens after dinner and to instruct me as to how I should go on.'

'That would hardly be a correct thing to do. You cannot go out into the gardens in the evening unescorted with a young man.'

'But he asked and secured his parents' permission.'

Good manners stopped Peter from saying cynically that he doubted if Gerald had obtained any such permission. He saw Miss Trumble watching them. 'Excuse me, Miss Moon,' he said. 'I have an idea.'

He joined Miss Trumble and told her of Gerald's invitation. 'You were right to tell me,' said Miss Trumble. 'Tell Miss Moon from me that it will be quite conventional if she is chaperoned. I elect myself her chaperone while she is here. Tell her we will both join Mr Parkes after dinner. I wonder how he will like that?' Peter smiled and returned to tell Tiffin of Miss Trumble's offer.

'I do not know how to thank you,' said Tiffin. 'I feel so *safe* with you beside me, Mr Bond.' Peter felt ten feet tall.

The duke was talking to Lizzie. 'Are you recovered from the ordeal of saving my life, Miss Lizzie?'

'I feel quite well, Your Grace, but I fear I shall have bad dreams.'

'What did Mr Parkes say to annoy you so much?'

'Nothing of consequence,' said Lizzie.

'Are you angry because he seems to have fallen for the charms of Miss Moon?'

'If he is set on breaking Miss Moon's heart as a way of providing himself with some excitement, then I shall be very angry indeed,' said Lizzie. 'I do not like philanderers.'

His eyes sparkled. 'Alas, you cannot like me. I am devastated.'

'I cannot imagine you philandering!'

'Do you find me staid and serious?'

'Your Grace, when I think of our previous conversation, I feel I have insulted you enough.'

He put her hand on his arm and began to walk down the long room with her. 'Advise me. What entertainment should I provide for these guests of mine? Or do you think I should pretend to fall ill and so be shot of them?'

'What of your marriage plans?'

'I fear I am destined to remain a bachelor.'

'You must try harder.'

'What if I have decided I wish to remain single?'

'Then that is your choice.'

Sarah Walters felt she could not bear it any longer. The duke had not even looked once in her direction. Somehow, she must distract his attention from Lizzie.

She moved until she was directly in their path, put her hand to her brow, and pretended to swoon in a dead faint at their feet.

Lizzie let out a gasp. The duke put his hand over her hand on his arm and held it in a firm clasp and guided her round Sarah's recumbent body, saying over his shoulder, 'Mrs Walters! Your daughter is unwell. Pray ring for the servants to remove her to her room, and should you need the physician, please summon him.' He turned back to Lizzie. 'To return to my earlier question, what entertainment should I supply?'

'Cards for the old people and dancing for the young,' said Lizzie. 'There is quite a good little orchestra in Hedgefield which plays at local assemblies.'

Sarah was being carried from the room by two strong footmen, followed by her parents and an anxious-looking Peter Bond. 'You did not believe she really fainted, did you?' asked Lizzie.

'No, I did not,' he said. 'But if she did, then she has her parents to look after her. I fear Mr Bond might be gullible enough to believe her really ill.'

'Did you see that?' hissed Verity to Celia. 'He is so taken up with Lizzie Beverley that he paid absolutely no attention when Miss Walters fainted at his feet.'

'Why do not we rescue him from death?' said Celia.

'And how do we do that?' asked Verity with contempt.

'We manufacture some event.'

Verity looked at her curiously. 'Such as what?'

'I have been thinking about it,' said Celia eagerly. 'We could perhaps wait until he is ready to go out riding. One of us will go up on the leads and drop a piece of masonry down on him and the other will push him clear.'

'It could work,' said Verity slowly. 'You could be stationed on the roof and I–'

'Why me on the roof? I thought of the idea. I should be the one to save him.'

'We will toss for it,' said Verity, fishing in her reticule and producing a crown piece. 'Heads I go on the roof, tails you do.'

'Oh, very well,' said Celia sulkily.

Verity tossed the coin. 'Tails,' she said triumphantly. 'You go on the roof.'

'Then you must think up a rescue for me to perform,' said Celia, feeling quite tearful. 'I think it most unfair that you should be the first to act the heroine when it was all my idea.'

Verity ignored her. 'We must have a word with him in private and find out when he plans to go out next.' She left Celia and joined the duke and Lizzie. To the duke's irritation, Lizzie murmured something and walked off to join Miss Moon.

'Do you often go riding early in the morning?' asked Verity.

'Quite often.'

'Tomorrow?'

He looked down at her impatiently. Gerald had joined Lizzie. What were they talking about?

'Yes, but too early for anyone else to be about. I leave at nine to ride to Hedgefield.'

To the duke's relief, dinner was announced.

At dinner the duke said to Miss Trumble, 'I am riding to Hedgefield in the morning.'

'For any particular reason?'

118

He smiled. 'Only to put a little distance between myself and my guests.'

'So it was all a mistake.'

'A very great mistake.' He hesitated. 'I may ask Miss Lizzie to accompany me. There can be nothing wrong in making an innocent expedition to a local town with Miss Lizzie.'

'Why do you wish her to go with you, Gervase?'

'She amuses me.'

Miss Trumble sat for a few moments in deep thought. 'Lizzie is in no danger of losing her heart to you,' she said at last. 'If there was any other gentleman in this party I considered a suitable beau for my Lizzie, then I would tell you to keep away from her and stop ruining her chances. I distrust Gerald Parkes. I fear his attentions to Miss Moon will be short-lived and he will soon turn his attentions back to Lizzie. You may go.'

'Thank you,' he said drily. 'Your time as a governess shows in that you manage to make me feel about ten years old.'

Miss Trumble smiled. 'I will tell Lizzie of your proposal so that she knows she has my approval.'

Sarah Walters lay in bed, a cloth soaked in cologne on her forehead. Her father's acid words rang in her ears. 'What possessed you to faint in that silly way? His Grace ain't interested in you. And why? Because you've left the field to Lizzie Beverley, that's why, with all your moping and maundering. If it hadn't been for the Beverley chit, you might have had a chance.'

Oh, why didn't Lizzie Beverley die? thought Sarah miserably.

To ease her mind, to take away the awful shame of that memory of the duke's paying absolutely no attention to her 'faint', she began to dream up ways of murdering Lizzie. An hour of hard dreaming intensified the idea that without Lizzie she, Sarah Walters, could become a duchess. Having, in her dreams, disposed of Lizzie, her dreams of that wedding to the duke came flooding back. But as she fell asleep, she plunged straight into a dream where she was at the duke's wedding but he was marrying Lizzie.

She awoke with a start. Something would have to be done.

Lizzie looked out nervously at a grey, misty morning. She had been so sure that the fine weather would last. She sensed approaching rain.

But she dressed with care, wearing the same riding outfit and hat. She had an older one she could have put on, but she felt that the new one was smarter.

With a feeling of nervous and happy anticipation, she walked down the stairs to meet the duke. It was not that she was in any way attracted to him, she told herself. It was just that she was only human and it was flattering to be selected as his companion a second time over the other eligible ladies in the house.

Celia was up on the roof, peering down into the swirling mist. She felt weak and dizzy. She was clutching a large square brick of Portland stone. If only the mist would clear.

It was too bad of Verity. It had all been her,

Celia's, idea, and she should be the one down there prepared to rescue the duke.

The shapes below her moved and changed in the mist. Horses neighed. Which figure was the duke? Then she heard Verity's voice. 'I declare I am a light sleeper. Why do I not change into my riding habit and join you?'

Treacherous girl, thought Celia furiously. That was not part of the plan.

Anger at Verity gave her strength as she heaved up the brick. Now all she wanted to do was get it over with and get down from this cold and dizzying perch.

Verity, a smile pinned on her face, wondered what was holding Celia up. She tried to delay the duke with further conversation, but Lizzie was already mounted. The duke swung himself up into the saddle, touched his hat to Verity, and he and Lizzie rode off down the drive.

And then Verity screamed as a brick hurtled down past her head, missing her by inches.

'What was that?' cried Lizzie. 'I heard a scream.'

'I neither know nor care,' shouted the duke above the drumming of the horses' hooves.

They rode on in silence after that through a dream countryside, bleached of all colour by the mist. At last he slowed and stopped on the rise above Hedgefield where they had stopped before. 'It will rain,' said Lizzie.

'It will not rain. You forget, I am a countryman. The sun will soon burn through the mist and we shall have a fine day.'

'And you forget I am a countrywoman, and it will rain!'

'Nonsense.'

'You are not always right, you know,' said Lizzie, feeling her hair coming out of its curl with the damp mist. 'Should we go on? The mist hides everything.'

'But I am sure you, the countrywoman, can find the road to Hedgefield in this mist.'

'Yes, but it is not very pleasant.'

'Your company makes it pleasant, Miss Lizzie.'

'You amaze me. Very well. Hedgefield it is. It is market day. There will be many people about.'

'What of it?'

'I will be seen with you and do not want to damage my reputation,' said Lizzie primly.

'Anyone seen with me has their reputation enhanced.'

Lizzie gasped. 'You are not even joking!'

'I am aware of my consequence.'

'How sad,' mocked Lizzie and spurred her horse.

He set out in pursuit of her flying figure, knowing that if he lost sight of her in the mist, he would probably lose his way.

They reached Hedgefield and left their horses at the Green Man and then walked through the gaily-coloured market stalls. Lizzie was greeted by many of the stall-holders and curious glances were thrown at the duke. And then a portly figure sailed through the mist and stopped in front of them.

'Lady Evans,' said Lizzie. She introduced the duke.

'We are acquainted,' said Lady Evans stiffly. 'Where is Miss Trumble?'

'At Mannerling,' said Lizzie. 'We are guests of the duke.'

'I am surprised Miss Trumble lets a young lady in her charge go unescorted,' said Lady Evans.

'I have her permission,' said the duke crossly.

'Yes, well, in the circumstances I am sure she could do little else if your mind was set on it,' retorted Lady Evans, who was aware of Miss Trumble's true identity. 'I shall call on Miss Trumble as soon as possible.'

The duke did not like the disapproving way she stared at Lizzie. He was tempted to say that he did not want callers and give her a set-down, but he remembered that this Lady Evans was an old friend of his aunt, and so he contented himself by saying coldly, 'As you wish. Come along, Lizzie.'

'Oh dear,' said Lizzie. 'How familiar of you!'

'What have I done?'

'You called me Lizzie.'

'Lady Evans will put the familiarity down to the great difference in our ages.'

'I had begun to forget that,' said Lizzie in a small voice. 'But you always say or do something to remind me of it.'

He stopped and looked down into her eyes. 'And that distresses you?'

'No, no. I mean, why should it?'

'Let us go to the inn for some refreshment.'

'We can hardly sit outside in this weather,' Lizzie pointed out.

'I will ask for a private parlour.'

The duke was used to his rank protecting him at all times from criticism and was blissfully un-aware that taking a young lady, known locally, to

123

a private parlour would cause a great deal of gossip.

Lady Evans had been following them at a little distance.

She had once had high hopes of securing a suitable marriage for the daughter of a friend of hers with an eligible man. But one of those wretched Beverley sisters had snatched the prize.

Lady Evans considered the Beverleys scheming and devious. She saw the duke and Lizzie go into the Green Man. She turned to her footman. 'Inquire discreetly what they are about.'

The footman returned after a few minutes and said, 'His Grace has engaged a private parlour.'

Lady Evans's face hardened. 'This is the outside of enough. Get the carriage. We are going to Mannerling.'

Gerald was wondering if he would ever have even a few moments alone with the increasingly desirable Tiffin. She was constantly supervised by Miss Trumble.

Therefore, when a certain Lady Evans was announced, who urgently desired to speak to the governess in private, he found Tiffin left unguarded.

'At last,' he said. 'I thought I would never speak to you again. What a dreary walk we had with that terrible old woman listening to every word.'

'Miss Trumble is very kind,' said Tiffin. Tiffin had been wondering when she could see Peter, but Peter had been very busy on the duke's behalf and was now closeted in the study.

'What do you want to talk to me about, sir?'

asked Tiffin politely.

Gerald spread his arms. 'Everything. Let us take a walk in the Long Gallery.'

Tiffin went with him. Perhaps Peter might come looking for her.

'I have something to tell you,' said Gerald as they walked along the gallery.

'Sir?'

'I have fallen in love with you.'

Tiffin blushed and her step faltered. 'I do not know what to say. My father is not here and my aunt is unwell. But perhaps you should approach my aunt, nonetheless, and ask her for her permission to pay your addresses to me.'

Gerald gave what he hoped was a rakish laugh. 'Ah, you are funning. Such a love as mine is not hidebound by the conventions.'

'A life like mine is very hidebound by the conventions,' said Tiffin. 'I am flattered by your declaration of love, but I fear I cannot return it.'

'My heart is broken.'

'I do not think you have a heart to break, Mr Parkes,' said Tiffin, remembering Lizzie's warning.

He knelt on one knee in front of her and took her hand in his and pressed a warm kiss on the back of it. 'Take pity on me, Miss Moon.'

Tiffin blushed again and snatched her hand away. 'I think I should see how my aunt fares.'

'I have frightened you, but all I wish is to love you.'

He rose to his feet. 'One kiss would ease the pain at my heart.'

He seized her in his arms.

Tiffin, despite the fragility of her appearance,

was a farmer's daughter and came from healthy country stock. With surprising strength and energy, she wrenched herself free and ran down the Long Gallery and headed straight for the study. She wrenched open the door, dived in, and slammed it behind her.

'Miss Moon!' cried Peter, getting to his feet.

'Oh, Mr Bond, if he comes, tell him I am not here. Send him away!'

'Who?'

'Mr Parkes.'

There was a knock at the door.

'Wait there,' commanded Peter.

He opened the door. 'Is Miss Moon here?' asked Gerald.

'Yes, she is and we have private business to discuss. Good day to you.' Peter shut the door firmly in Gerald's face.

He turned around. 'I was just about to take a rest from work. Shall I ring for tea?'

'Thank you,' said Tiffin shyly. 'I should like that above all things.'

Lizzie enjoyed her chat with the duke in the private parlour. They had discussed books and plays and the state of the nation. She only became aware of the unconventionality of their behaviour after the duke had said reluctantly that they should take their leave. As they made their way down the stairs, a housemaid bobbed a curtsy, but before she lowered her eyes Lizzie saw a sort of salacious curiosity in them.

'I should never have let you entertain me in a private parlour,' she said, as they went outside. 'I fear my reputation is quite ruined.'

'My actions are above reproach,' said the duke loftily.

'Oh, you are so *arrogant.*' Lizzie stamped her foot. 'It will be all over Hedgefield, and our servant, Barry, will be shortly returned from Bath. He will get to hear of it and he will tell your aunt.'

'I am not interested in the tittle-tattle of a bunch of peasants.'

'Do you never stop to think of my position? What if some gentleman should be interested in me and get to hear that I spent some time in a private parlour with the Duke of Severnshire.'

'I do not, and have never had, the reputation of a rake, Miss Lizzie.'

'You have now,' said Lizzie gloomily, 'and I am the whore of Babylon.'

'I see what it is,' he said, his eyes cold. 'I had forgot about the Beverley ambition. You are trying to force me to propose to you.'

Lizzie's face flamed with anger. 'You are insufferable. I do not want to marry a creaking old fool like you!'

'You are insolent!'

'And you are so rigidly armoured in arrogance and self-consequence that you are nigh inhuman!'

Their horses were brought round. The duke threw Lizzie up into the saddle with such force that she had to grasp the pommel to save herself from tumbling over the other side.

Her words burnt and hurt. He would like to have ridden away from her but the mist was thick and he felt sure he could not find the way back to

Mannerling on his own.

And then it began to rain heavily. Lizzie stopped and dismounted under a stand of trees and he joined her. 'I am not dressed for this weather,' she said crossly, 'and my new riding habit will be ruined.'

'It looks set for the day,' he said bleakly.

She gave a tired sigh. 'Well, I don't want to be trapped here with you all day.' A little sob was wrenched from her and one large tear slid down her cheek.

'Lizzie,' he said, wondering. 'Miss Beverley!' He took off his riding gloves. One long finger reached out to that tear.

'Leave me alone!' Lizzie jerked her face away.

'I have distressed you, indeed,' he said contritely. 'Come, let us be friends and put this sorry misunderstanding behind us. You worry too much about that private parlour. Believe me, people will think nothing of it.'

She gave him a watery smile. 'I fear you really do not understand the gossip that is rife in a country place. Let us go. Miss Trumble will be becoming anxious.'

He put his arms at her waist to throw her up into the saddle. He looked down into her face. She was still upset and her lips trembled. He gently kissed her on the lips. They felt warm and sweet. He suddenly wanted to stay where he was and go on kissing her, but with a great effort he helped her up into the saddle and then mounted himself. They rode off into the rain.

By the time they reached the long drive which led up to Mannerling, Lizzie was soaked to the skin, but she felt no physical discomfort because her mind was in such a turmoil.

The duke had dried himself and changed when a footman called to say that Miss Trumble and Lady Evans wished to speak to him as soon as possible.

'Where are they?'

'In the Green Saloon, your grace.'

The duke entered the Green Saloon. As both elderly ladies rose and curtsied to him, he looked at their severe and disapproving faces and felt like a boy who has been caught stealing apples.

'Sit down, Gervase,' said Miss Trumble. 'Lady Evans is called with some shocking intelligence.'

'I trust nothing ill has happened to your family?' The duke flipped up his coat-tails and sat down.

'I believe you engaged a private parlour at the Green Man and there you entertained Lizzie,' said Miss Trumble.

He raised his thin eyebrows. 'Yes?'

'Had you no care for the girl's reputation?' barked Lady Evans.

'We wished some refreshment and I could hardly entertain her in the tap,' said the duke.

'The inn servants will gossip,' said Miss Trumble, 'and that gossip will spread out throughout the county.'

'I did nothing wrong and I do not like to be interrogated like this,' said the duke. 'Now if that is all...?'

'No, it is not all,' said Miss Trumble in an exasperated voice. 'What are we to do to repair Lizzie's reputation?'

129

'You will next be suggesting that I marry her,' said the duke.

'Yes.' That one quiet word from Miss Trumble dropped into the quietness of the room like a stone.

Rain dripped monotonously from the eaves, a log shifted in the fire, and the clocks of Mannerling ticked and chattered and tocked, racing away the minutes and hours.

The Beverleys should not have such a prize, thought Lady Evans. 'Now, now, Letitia is joking,' said Lady Evans. 'I am sure there is no need to go to such extremes. I suggest Lizzie be sent away to one of her sisters, preferably the one in Ireland, until everyone has forgotten the gossip. She is too young and heedless for you, Duke, and I am sure your aunt will forgive me for pointing out that the Beverleys are not up to your weight.'

'Lizzie is too generous and warm-hearted to be forced into a marriage she does not want,' said Miss Trumble. 'But I would suggest an engagement, to be terminated after a few months.'

The duke was about to contemptuously dismiss this suggestion, but then in a flash he realized it had advantages. He would be free of the expectations of the other guests and their families. Lizzie was bright and amusing. He was sure the idea of an engagement would intrigue her. She would see the funny side of it.

'Very well,' said the duke. 'If Miss Lizzie will agree to a few months' engagement, so be it.'

'If you will take my advice,' said Lady Evans heavily, 'you will get her to sign something. Have you met Lady Beverley? That family will have you

130

in court for breach of promise, I assure you.'

'That is going too far,' protested Miss Trumble. 'I will guarantee Lizzie's integrity.'

'Let's put it to her,' said Lady Evans cynically.

When Lizzie entered, she looked curiously at the three of them. 'Sit down, child,' said Miss Trumble.

Lizzie sat down. Lady Evans surveyed her sourly. That red hair! It practically lit up the room! And those odd green eyes sparkling in that thin face.

'Lizzie,' began Miss Trumble gently, 'we fear His Grace has damaged your reputation.'

Those green eyes of Lizzie's flickered towards the duke. 'It was only a kiss, and no one saw us.'

Lady Evans and Miss Trumble glared at the duke who, for once in his life, looked nonplussed.

'This is worse than we thought,' exclaimed Lady Evans.

'I did not know of any kiss,' said Miss Trumble. 'Are your affections seriously engaged after all, Gervase?'

'I have become ... fond ... of the child, that is all,' said the duke stiffly.

'The fact remains that you entertained her in a private parlour and your great rank, instead of protecting her name, can only do the opposite. Your assignation with Lizzie – and that is how it will appear – was cause of a great deal of harmful gossip to her reputation. To that end, I have a suggestion. Lizzie, you and Gervase will announce your engagement, and after a few months, when the scandal has died down, you will break that engagement.'

Lizzie's first furious thought was: How dare he

131

kiss me and then say he was only fond of me? How dare he call me a child?

'I do not want to be engaged to His Grace,' she said primly, although her eyes had a dangerous sparkle. 'What if some suitable *young* man should take my fancy? No one will believe I have rejected a duke. All will say that *he* terminated the engagement.'

'I shall look suitably heartbroken,' said the duke drily.

'You must be guided by me,' said Miss Trumble. 'Have I ever guided you wrong, Lizzie?'

Lizzie stared at her shoes.

Then she raised her eyes and looked at the duke. 'This suits you very well, does it not? In this way, you will be rid of your guests.'

'Agreed. May I point out, Miss Lizzie,' said the duke, 'that your apparent securing of my affections can do your social consequence nothing but good?'

'I think,' said Lizzie coldly, 'that that must be about the most pompous, arrogant statement I have ever heard.'

'Manners!' cried Lady Evans, shocked.

'I do think, Gervase,' said Miss Trumble, 'that you are being high-handed over this. Lady Evans and I will leave you alone for ten minutes and I suggest you put your proposal in a more ... friendly ... manner.'

Both ladies rose and left, Lady Evans with obvious reluctance.

Lizzie and the duke eyed each other like adversaries.

The thought that he would be free of his guests

prompted the duke to adopt a conciliatory manner. 'If you look at it this way,' he said, 'it would not be all that bad a thing.'

'Have you any idea the effect such news will have on my mother?' asked Lizzie. 'For a few months she will be in alt and then she will be cast down again when the engagement is broken.'

'Then we shall tell her of our arrangement.'

'She would never agree to such an arrangement. The way I see it,' said Lizzie, 'is that there is no advantage to me.'

'According to my aunt, your reputation is ruined.'

'Fiddle. Now I come to think of it, I am well enough known to all in the countryside. I am a Beverley,' said Lizzie with a hauteur that matched the duke's own.

He gave a slight shrug. 'I am tired of arguing about this. If you do not wish the arrangement, so be it.'

Lady Evans and Miss Trumble were summoned. Miss Trumble's fine eyes sparkled with anger. 'You are being very silly, Lizzie. But you will soon find out the extent to which your reputation has been ruined. As for you, Gervase. As your intentions towards Lizzie seem all that is dishonourable, I would suggest you do not go out again with her alone or kiss her.'

'Gladly,' said the duke sourly.

'You are a silly little girl,' exclaimed Lady Evans.

Lizzie sank into a low curtsy and left the room, her head held high.

But the gossip about her spread out from Hedge-

133

field to the Mannerling servants and so to the ears of the guests. 'There you are!' cried Verity to Celia. 'He had no real interest in the chit at all. Only dalliance. She is unsuitable to his rank.'

Sarah Walters turned the news over in her mind. Perhaps the duke had been trying to make her jealous! For now Sarah lived totally in fantasy. Every time the duke looked in her direction, Sarah saw burning passion.

Gerald Parkes was at first startled by the news and then delighted. His pursuit of Miss Moon had failed. But if Lizzie Beverley cared so little for her reputation, then it stood to reason that she was easy game.

Lizzie was aware of the charged atmosphere in the drawing-room that evening. Celia and Verity were giving her sly looks. They had been friendly for a brief period before, trying to get to know her better, trying to find out what there was about her that had attracted the duke, but now they felt infinitely superior to her. The Chumleys, that normally friendly and cheerful couple, did not answer Lizzie's cheerful greeting, in fact they looked right through her. Colonel and Mrs Parkes called Gerald sharply to their side when he would have joined Lizzie.

Peter Bond was absent and Lizzie felt quite friendless. Miss Trumble was of no help at all, seemingly blind to Lizzie's plight.

Only Miss Moon tried to be friendly but in such a gentle, embarrassed way that her behaviour more than that of the others brought home to Lizzie the extent of her shame.

After dinner, she could bear the atmosphere no

longer. She pleaded a headache and left the room.

The duke noticed that after a few moments, Gerald Parkes slid out of the room as well. It would be just like that young fool to decide that Lizzie could be had by anybody.

Colonel Parkes was talking to him about military matters. The duke listened courteously but he began to become very worried indeed.

Lizzie was sitting at her toilet-table brushing out her red hair when there came a scratching at her door. 'Come in,' she called, expecting it to be Miss Trumble.

Gerald came in, a broad grin on his face.

Lizzie swung round, dropping the brush in her surprise. 'What are you doing here?'

Gerald shut the door behind him and lunged forward. 'Your hair is pretty.' He picked up a lock of it.

Lizzie angrily jerked her head away.

His hand fell to her shoulder and caressed it. 'Don't be so missish with me, sweeting,' he said. 'Let's sample a little of what you have been giving so freely to Severnshire.'

Lizzie jumped to her feet and pushed him away. She ran for the bell-rope by the fireplace but he grabbed her gown and jerked her back and caught her in his arms.

'Leave me alone,' shouted Lizzie.

The door swung open and the duke walked in. He seized Gerald by the collar and pulled him back, and then punched him full on the nose. 'How dare you lay hands on my fiancée!' he shouted.

Gerald pulled a handkerchief from his pocket and dabbed at the blood streaming from his nose.

'I did not know she was your fiancée,' he said when he could. 'It's all over the county that she's your slut.'

'If it weren't for the respect I have for your parents,' said the duke, 'I would call you out. Get out of here and make your arrangements with your parents for a speedy departure.'

When Gerald had left, Lizzie sank down on a chair and buried her face in her hands.

'I was wrong,' said the duke stiffly. 'Come, Lizzie, we must be engaged. The damage to your reputation must be repaired, and quickly, too.'

Lizzie uncovered her face and looked up at him miserably. 'I suppose there is no alternative?'

'I am afraid not.'

'Then let it be so,' said Lizzie wearily. 'But we must not tell Mama the truth of the matter. I could not bear the recriminations.'

'May I suggest that we try to look as if we are fond of each other?'

'I will try,' said Lizzie bleakly.

'How is your headache?'

'I didn't have one. The atmosphere of shame and blame in the drawing-room was too much for me.'

He held out his hand. 'Come. Let us shake on it, Lizzie Beverley.'

She put out her hand and he covered it in a warm clasp. Then he bent and kissed her on the forehead.

'Do not look so miserable,' he said. 'It is not a death sentence.'

'It is this house,' said Lizzie. 'It makes terrible things happen.'

'It is only a house.' But he remembered again that reflection in the mirror.

Lizzie shuddered. 'I feel in my bones that something terrible is about to happen.'

'Your nerves are overset. Go to sleep. Things will look better in the morning. Mr Bond will send off the announcement of our betrothal to the newspapers.'

Lizzie gave him a shaky smile. 'We shall hear Mama screaming with delight all the way from Bath.'

'We shall announce our engagement before dinner tomorrow. I would suggest that we appear a loving couple and so quench all hope. Do you think you can manage that?'

'I will try,' said Lizzie, 'but it will be difficult.'

'Am I such a monster?'

'Rather forbidding.'

'You did not think so when I kissed you.'

'I was taken by surprise. Oh, go away, Your Grace, and let me rest and get over the shock of all this.'

He bowed and left. She had looked very pretty with her hair down. He would need to be extremely warm and affectionate to her on the morrow so that the engagement would be believed. The thought of being warm and affectionate to Lizzie Beverley made his heart lift as he strode from the west wing.

Then he stopped. There was the sound of tinkling chandelier crystals. He stood on the landing and looked down into the Great Hall. The chandelier had not been replaced. Great candelabra now burnt in the corners of the hall. But the tinkling went on, mocking, almost challenging in its sound.

He decided to get the servants to investigate in the morning. Someone was playing tricks on him.

Farmer Moon glared at the letter which had arrived by hand from his daughter in reply to one he himself had sent the day before. In his letter, he had asked whether she had managed to attract the attention of the duke. In her reply his daughter had written that the duke was too far above her but that his secretary, Mr Bond, had been all that was kind.

A mere secretary! The farmer decided that it was time he called on his daughter and told her what he thought of her lowly ambition. He wrote her a letter saying he would be calling on her on the morrow to give her a lecture. Was a daughter of his who had received the best education going to throw herself away on a secretary? If she did not make a push to secure the duke's affections, then he would see to it she was kept on a diet of bread and water. He then sanded and sealed the letter and sent it back by hand.

Tiffin, on receiving this letter, was thrown into a panic. She could not show it to Peter Bond, for it would show her interest in him and he might be shocked. Tiffin also knew her aunt was perfectly well able now to make the journey home and was only pretending to be ill so as to prolong their visit.

She wandered dismally out into the gardens,

138

now glistening under the morning sun.

Gerald, who was moodily striding up and down and beheading flowers with his cane and plotting revenge, saw her and walked quickly up to her. 'You look so distressed, Miss Moon. If there is anything I can do to help you, I am your servant to command.'

'No one can help me,' said Tiffin in a dreary little voice. 'My father is coming tomorrow to lecture me. He has run mad. He wants me to marry the duke.'

'That's out of the question,' said Gerald savagely. 'He told me last night he is engaged to Lizzie Beverley.'

'Then Aunt and Papa will say I have failed. Papa says he will put me on bread and water.' She gave a pathetic little sob. She did not want to tell Gerald that it was her apparent admiration of Peter that had prompted her father into his forthcoming visit.

Gerald had a wonderful plan. He would offer to rescue this little charmer and take her away with him. He would tell his parents that he had quarrelled with the duke over some trivial matter and thought he should leave ahead of them. Tiffin, distressed and vulnerable, looked infinitely desirable in the morning sunlight.

'I will rescue you,' he said. 'I have fallen in love with you. Oh, I know you have been told my intentions are dishonourable, but I love and respect you. We could leave tomorrow before your father's arrival. Say you will come with me.'

Tiffin looked at him, wide-eyed. He was not so handsome that morning, his nose being swollen and red, but his blue eyes were kind and sincere. She thought he was offering her an elopement. He was of good family. Once the marriage was a reality, her father would come about. She did not love him, she loved Peter Bond. But Mr Bond would never run away with her, and in any case, the duke would not allow him to marry. If she stayed, her father would make a vulgar scene, and her aunt would rant and rave.

'I do not love you, Mr Parkes, but I am deeply grateful to you. I could come to love you.'

'That is enough for me,' said Gerald fervently.

'Is it far to Scotland?' asked Tiffin timidly.

'Scotland? Oh, Gretna,' said Gerald, thinking with a pang of guilt that this chit really expected him to marry her over the anvil at the blacksmith's at Gretna. 'Well, as to that, I thought we'd go somewhere and make some plans. But you must not breathe a word about this to anybody. Promise?'

'I promise,' said Tiffin in a low voice.

'Then take only one bandbox and meet me outside the main door at six in the morning. No one will be about. Should any servant question you, however, you must say that I am taking you to visit your father.'

'Very well. I am so frightened.'

'I will save you,' said Gerald, striking his breast. 'Only you must not tell anyone, anyone at all.'

The company met in the drawing-room for dinner after a long and boring day during which none of them had seen anything of the duke. He had given up any idea of entertaining them. When they were all gathered, he went up to Lizzie and took her hand in his.

'I wish to announce that Miss Lizzie Beverley and I are engaged to be married,' he said. 'Wish us well.'

Servants came in and carried around trays of champagne. The duke pressed Lizzie's hand hard. 'Look as if you love me,' he hissed.

At first he thought she was not going to comply, but she suddenly raised a glowing face to his. He raised her hand to his lips and kissed it.

Then the room was rent by a scream. Transfixed, all eyes turned to Sarah Walters. 'You compromised him,' she shouted. 'You stole him away from me.' Then she burst into noisy tears.

'Please take her away immediately,' said Miss Trumble to the furious squire and his startled wife.

The Chumleys bustled forward to offer their congratulations as a weeping Sarah was led from the room. Peter felt covered in shame. It was all his fault that Sarah had been invited. How could he have been such a fool? He had tried to speak to Tiffin, but she had answered him in monosyllables. He had thought she was becoming fond of him, but there was no longer anything in her manner to suggest such a thing. Verity and Celia offered their congratulations, both with thin smiles fixed on their faces. Their parents did the same but Verity's father, the earl, was heard to say loudly, 'Well, I for one am set on leaving. This visit has been a deuced waste of time.'

As Celia's parents began to say that they must also make preparations to leave, Miss Trumble wondered how they could bear to make their ambitions so blatant. All at once, Miss Trumble missed Barry and wondered if he had returned from Bath.

It was an awkward dinner. This time Lizzie was led in by the duke and seated at his right hand. But the duke smiled at her, his silvery eyes lit up – apparently – with love. Lizzie, at first dismayed to be involved in what she privately damned as 'such a farce', remembered her part of the bargain and smiled back at the duke, trying to fight down an odd little longing which made her wish that his affection were real.

She usually only drank water at meals, but this time she drank wine to help her in her act of being the loving fiancée.

Miss Trumble watched them sadly, thinking them a pair of excellent actors, and wondering what on earth was going to become of little Lizzie Beverley now. When the engagement was terminated, Miss Trumble decided to revert to her real name and status and take a house in London and bring Lizzie out herself.

Celia and Verity were barely speaking. Celia blamed Verity for having 'forced' her to go up on that roof, and Verity blamed Celia for having nearly killed her and was rapidly coming to the conclusion that it had been a deliberate attempt on her life.

The squire and his wife were absent from the dinner-table. The squire had expended his rage on his wife and daughter to such effect that he was quite exhausted.

After dinner no one seemed inclined to stay,

up, playing cards or chatting. One by one they made their excuses and left.

The duke walked Lizzie to her room. 'You did well tonight,' he said. 'One would think you actually liked me.'

'I do not dislike you,' said Lizzie. 'You are also a good actor.'

'Would you believe me if I said I was not acting?'

Lizzie looked up at him. In the shadowy light of the corridor he looked a grand and formidable figure armoured in evening dress, the diamond of his stick-pin buried in the snowy folds of his cravat. His hooded eyes were inscrutable.

'No,' she said bluntly.

He gave a little laugh and kissed her cheek. 'The way they were all going on tonight, we should be shot of them tomorrow.'

'I am worried about little Miss Moon. She appeared in sore distress. I hope Mr Parkes has not been worrying her.'

'Probably only that dreadful aunt of hers. Parkes will not trouble her. If he touches you again, I shall kill him. Good night, Lizzie.'

'Good night, Your Grace.'

'You may call me Gervase.'

'Good night, Gervase.'

He seemed to loom over her for a moment and her breath became rapid and she lowered her eyes. But when she looked up again, he was striding off down the corridor.

SIX

A taste for drink, combined with gout,
Had doubled him up for ever.

W. S. GILBERT

Miss Trumble could not sleep. She had begun to think Lizzie and her nephew were very well suited, but was afraid of hoping too much. There was a restless, malignant air to the great house that night. She put her head down on the pillow and tried to compose herself for sleep, but, faintly to her ears, came the sound of weeping. She thought it might be the house playing tricks on her senses, but decided to go and investigate. She called at Sarah's bedchamber first, but that young lady was deep in sleep. She stood for a moment, irresolute, and then she remembered how distressed little Miss Moon had looked. She walked along to Miss Moon's bedchamber and listened outside, hearing the sounds of sobbing. She opened the door and went in.

Tiffin was not in bed. She was sitting in a chair by the fire, crying dismally.

'Now, then, child,' said Miss Trumble gently. 'Whatever ails you can be mended if you talk about it.'

Tiffin scrubbed at her eyes with an already sodden handkerchief and said in a choked voice, 'I gave my word not to talk about it.'

144

Miss Trumble pulled a chair up next to her. 'If the something you gave your word not to talk about is causing you so much fright and distress, then that something must be very wrong indeed. You are a good girl, and as far as I can judge, a moral one. You are sorely in need of a friend. I am that friend, Miss Moon.'

Tiffin gave a shuddering sob and then hung her head. 'It is Papa,' she said. 'He has great ambitions for me. I wrote to him and said the duke was too far above me and that I was ... interested ... in Mr Bond. He replied that he had not paid for an expensive education for me in a Bath seminary that I might throw myself away on a mere secretary. To that end, he plans to arrive tomorrow to read me the riot act.'

Miss Trumble's worried face cleared. 'Then he will have me to deal with. You are not alone.'

Tiffin's large eyes swam with tears again. 'There is worse.'

'Out with it!' commanded Miss Trumble bracingly.

'He will be so angry if he knows I have told you. Mr Parkes wishes me to elope with him in the morning while everyone else is still abed.'

'Did he mention marriage?'

'Not precisely. But what else could he mean? I asked him if it was a long way to Scotland.'

'To which Mr Parkes replied?'

'He said something like we should go somewhere first to plan things.'

Miss Trumble took a deep breath. 'This is very wrong. You are a perfectly respectable young lady, and were Mr Parkes's ambitions honourable, then

145

he would have consulted his parents and then asked your aunt and your father for your hand in marriage. You have nothing to fear from your father. Not only will I deal with him, but Mr Bond will do so as well.'

'But he will tell Mr Bond of my interest in him,' wailed Tiffin.

'Listen to me. You are not going anywhere tomorrow and as you are a timid little thing, your father will be told by me that you are unwell and unfit to see him. I will return shortly and tell you of my other plans.'

Tiffin gave her a watery smile. 'You are so strong and so resolute. You must have only contempt for me.'

'The only contempt I feel at this moment is for Mr Parkes. Wait here.'

Miss Trumble went straight to the duke's room. He was not asleep, but sitting reading by the fire.

'Gervase,' said Miss Trumble. 'Here's a coil.' She told him of Gerald's attempted seduction of Tiffin.

The duke put down his book and stood up. 'Mr Parkes is going to be made to feel very sorry for himself. Let me ring for Mr Bond. I have noticed my secretary's feelings have left Miss Walters and become attached to Miss Moon, but we shall see.'

'You would allow him to marry?'

'Yes, I have thought of it and do not see how marriage would interfere with his duties.'

Peter was sent for and the whole matter explained. Miss Trumble, with amusement, noticed that the news that pretty Tiffin had a tendre for him was making him look quite elated.

'Her father is descending on us tomorrow, Mr

146

Bond,' said the duke. 'My aunt and I will deal with him. You may court Miss Moon if you wish. As I have pointed out to my aunt, I see no reason why you cannot be married and continue your duties to me.'

Peter thanked him, but then said, 'Do you wish me to rouse Mr and Mrs Parkes?'

'No,' said the duke slowly, 'I would like to see Mr Parkes well and truly humiliated. I think I have a plan.'

Gerald had spent a restless night. He had tossed and turned, plagued with fears that Tiffin might have confided in someone. It was a relief to at last prepare to depart. He had to go to the stables first and ask for a carriage to be brought round to the door. He could not ask for a travelling carriage, for that would occasion too much curiosity. But then, he did not plan to go very far.

The sleepy head groom showed no curiosity whatsoever. The carriage would be outside the door at six. It was an open carriage, but the morning was fine, with shafts of sunlight striking through the lime trees which bordered the drive.

Again he had a nagging little feeling of guilt. The morning was so sweet and innocent – birds singing out their hearts to the rising sun, dew glistening on flowers and grass. But he pushed the thought away. Gerald's parents had not spoilt him, but his incredibly good looks and a too-lenient tutor on the Grand Tour most certainly had. Gerald had enjoyed a time of great sexual licence in Italy and had begun to think that morals were something the upper classes pretended to have but only the lower classes practised.

He stood impatiently outside the door. The carriage was brought round, a light curricle pulled by only one horse. He looked impatiently at his watch. And then the door behind him opened and a slim, heavily veiled figure came through carrying a bandbox.

'Get in the carriage,' he urged, 'and let us make all speed before we are discovered.'

A nod of the head. He helped her into the carriage and then climbed in and picked up the reins and soon they were bowling down the long drive. He planned to make it to the nearest large town of Barminster and find a room in a posting-house and take it from there.

He was so intent on putting as many miles as possible between himself and Mannerling that he did not slow his pace to converse or ask his companion how she fared. He was amused by the thick black veil she wore and wondered where she had managed to find it or if she was always prepared for a funeral.

At last they arrived in Barminster and he drove straight into the yard of The George. He decided to engage a private parlour and then get around to the tricky business of moving her to a bedchamber later.

It was only nine o'clock in the morning, hardly the time of day to ply her with wine, but he might be prepared to get her to share a jug of ale with breakfast.

To his relief, she stood beside him silently while he engaged a private parlour 'for myself and my wife'.

First hurdle over.

He ordered breakfast to be sent up. Once inside the private parlour, he tried to take her in his arms, but she whispered, 'Not yet.'

The servants soon arrived with breakfast, but his companion sat there as silently and heavily veiled as ever.

Then, when the servants had retired, to his exasperation she began to eat heartily, tucking mouthfuls of food up under her veil.

'There is no need for such secrecy any more, my sweeting,' he said. 'Pray remove your veil.'

A shake of the head was his only answer.

He was nervous, angry, and nonplussed all at once. There was no atmosphere of timidity or worry about her situation that he would have expected from such a shy girl as Tiffin.

'Take off your veil ... *now!*' he commanded.

'Shan't,' said an amused voice from under the veil.

His eyes narrowed. The voice had a country burr and Tiffin had none.

He found the palms of his hands were sweating.

He walked round the table and ripped off that veil and hat. A cheeky face under a red-gold mop of curls looked up at him.

'Who are you?' cried Gerald.

'Lamp-boy from Mannerling, Freddy Potter,' said the boy laconically. Mannerling, like other great and rich establishments, had so many oil-lamps that a boy was employed for the sole purpose of trimming, filling and cleaning the lamps.

Gerald drew back his fist, his face flaming with fury.

149

'I wouldn't do that or it'll be the worse for you,' said Freddy.

'I am going to beat you within an inch of your life,' howled Gerald.

'And I'll scream me head off and cry rape,' said Freddy, 'and they'll all come running and wonder o' wonders, it's a boy, and you'll be damned as a backgammon player. Raping females is one thing, raping boys is a time in the stocks.'

Gerald's fist fell to his side. The awful truth of what the boy had just said was borne in on him. He turned quite white. 'Who was behind this plot?' he asked.

'His Grace,' said Freddy. He wiped a piece of bread round the remains of egg on his plate, wiped his mouth on the tablecloth, stood up and walked to the door. He put on his hat and veil. 'Don't let your breakfast get cold, sir,' he said mockingly.

Freddy went quickly down the stairs and commanded the inn servants to bring 'her' carriage round. The horse would be tired, he thought, but he could drive very slowly and easily back to Mannerling.

Gerald sat alone over his nearly untasted food, burning with humiliation. He could not go back. He could not face his parents. He was lucky in that he had a generous inheritance from a late uncle. He was not dependent on his parents for money. He thought of Rome, of the sunshine, of the easy immoral life. He would call at his bank in London and then make his way to the coast. But for a small revenge, he would sell that carriage and horse before he left Barminster.

He, of course, found both carriage and horse gone.

Farmer Moon had been feeling as grand as a lord when he left his farm. His sturdy girth was encased in a morning coat of Bath superfine, his shirt-points were so starched that they cut into his florid cheeks, a gold watch the size of a turnip hung from his watch-chain, along with a selection of seals and fobs.

He had never been to Mannerling before, not even on the days when the locals were invited. As the carriage moved up the long drive and the graceful building that was Mannerling hove into view, he gave a little gulp. He had heard through local gossip that the duke had bought it on a whim to add to his other residences and had expected something more in the lines of a hunting-box. He had discounted tales of the grandeur of Mannerling, thinking country people were easily impressed. But the splendid lines of the building, the porticoed entrance with two tall liveried footmen already waiting, took him aback.

But, he braced himself with the thought, he had every right to call. His daughter and sister were guests of this duke, were they not?

He had an uneasy feeling that the liveries of the servants were better tailored than his own coat, of which he had been so very proud when he struggled into it that morning.

The footman helped him down from his carriage. He had been driving himself, fancying himself as a good whip. A groom went to the horse's head but did not lead horse and carriage to the stables, a sign that his visit was not expected to be of any long duration.

Then he was in the Great Hall of Mannerling. He gawped up at the painted ceilings and then ahead at the double staircase down which a butler who looked as grand as an archbishop was descending.

He had a struggle to extract his card case from his waistcoat pocket, for his waistcoat, like his coat, was very tight. He handed the butler his card.

The butler held the card with the tips of his gloved fingers and looked silently at the farmer.

'I am come to see my daughter, Miss Moon,' said Mr Moon testily.

The butler gave a slight bow and went back up the staircase, oh, so very slowly, his very back seeming to imply that no one could possibly be in a hurry to greet such an undistinguished guest.

Mr Moon took out a handkerchief and mopped his brow. Four footmen stood at attention on either side of the staircase and regarded him solemnly.

At last the butler came back, still with that very slow gait. He inclined his head. 'Be so good as to follow me, sir,' he said.

Farmer Moon let out a little puff of relief. He had begun to entertain the awful thought that he might be sent away.

But the thought that he was going to see his own daughter gave him courage. Tiffin was a pretty girl, but the ambitious farmer thought she was a great beauty. His wife had had only indifferent looks and he saw in this only daughter a means to get on in society.

But when the double doors of the Yellow Saloon were thrown open and he was ushered in, his heart sank. It was a very large room with little islands of furniture dotted here and there.

A tall, imposing man was standing by the fireplace, an elderly lady was seated on a sofa and an unexceptionable young man in coat and breeches of correct black was standing by a window.

'Be seated, Moon,' said the tall man. 'I am Severnshire. May I present Miss Trumble, a friend of the family? And my secretary, Mr Bond.'

'Oh, you're Bond, are you?' said Mr Moon.

'It was Mr Bond who rescued your daughter and your sister,' said the duke severely, and Mr Moon muttered a gruff 'Thank'ee'. Then he looked around. 'Where is my daughter?'

'Your daughter,' said the lady called Miss Trumble, 'is indisposed.'

'What? What's up with her?'

'A nervous crisis caused by the news of your visit,' said Miss Trumble severely. 'Miss Moon feels she has failed you.'

He goggled at her.

'Yes, failed you,' went on Miss Trumble. 'I gather that you expected her to marry Severnshire.'

Put like that, it now seemed like the height of impertinence. Farmer Moon began to bluster while the sweat of embarrassment ran down his red face. 'Look'ee here,' he said desperately, 'I don't know what my Tiffin has been telling you, but all I wanted to do was to stop her chasing after – you will beg my pardon, Your Grace – your secretary.'

153

'And what is your objection to my secretary?' demanded the duke awfully. 'Mr Bond is of the Cambridgeshire Bonds.'

'I didn't know,' said Mr Moon wretchedly. 'I mean, he's only a secretary.'

'You must not discuss Mr Bond as if he were not in the room,' said Miss Trumble.

Farmer Moon mulishly stood his ground. 'He's a servant and can't marry.'

'He is my right-hand man,' said the duke, 'and when he marries, he will have a house on my estate and a reasonable competence.'

'I didn't know that,' said Mr Moon weakly.

'I am sure you really did not expect me to pay my addresses to your daughter, charming as she is,' went on the duke.

Miss Trumble felt a pang of sympathy for this farmer. She almost felt like saying, 'Why not? Miss Moon is an exceptionable young lady.' The farmer was a bully and yet, as Miss Trumble knew, any parent with a pretty daughter could be slightly unbalanced in this wicked age of social climbing and snobbery. But she continued to look at him accusingly.

The farmer's brain was trying to assimilate what the duke had said about his secretary. It now appeared that if his Tiffin married this secretary, she would after all be a lady of consequence, and since the duke appeared to value this young man so highly, then he, Farmer Moon, would be on calling terms with a duke.

'I seem to have been hasty and rash in my judgement. 'Pologize,' he said.

He looked directly at Peter. 'Do you want to

marry my daughter?'

Peter walked forward. 'I would like your permission to pay my addresses to her.'

By now, the farmer would have done anything to please this terrifying, autocratic duke and this stately old lady whose bright eyes made him feel such a fool.

'Oh, very well,' he said. 'You have my blessing, my boy.'

The frigid atmosphere in the room visibly thawed. Miss Trumble smiled, a charming smile, and said, 'You will join us for tea,' and rang the bell.

The duke then pulled a chair up next to the one on which the farmer was perched and began to talk knowledgeably of crops and fertilizers. Gradually, Mr Moon began to relax. At last he asked humbly, 'May I see my daughter?'

Miss Trumble rose. 'I will see how she fares.'

By the time Miss Trumble led Tiffin into the drawing room, Mr Moon was chatting easily with the duke and Peter, now saving up every morsel of this grand visit to tell his neighbours.

After clumsily embracing his daughter, he said, 'I have given Mr Bond my blessing.'

And poor Tiffin, who had no idea that Peter had any serious intentions towards her, suddenly looked so radiant that in that one moment a pretty girl turned into a very beautiful young woman.

'I think Miss Trumble and I will take you somewhere else and leave your daughter and Mr Bond for a few moments,' said the duke.

The farmer was led off into an even grander saloon while Tiffin shyly faced Peter. 'You did not

155

do this just to save me from my father's wrath?' she asked.

Peter took her hand. 'No, I did it because I have fallen in love with you.'

He took her in his arms and kissed her gently. Then he said, 'I made a very sad mistake bringing Miss Walters here, but I met you, and that makes up for everything. Thanks to my master's engagement to Miss Beverley, our guests will soon be gone and we can be comfortable again.'

After matters had been explained to Aunt Bertha, she crossly said she was suddenly well and wished to go home and take Tiffin with her. But she was told that Tiffin, with her father's permission, was to remain and be chaperoned by Miss Trumble. Miss Trumble heaved a sigh of relief. The Chumleys were leaving; Mr and Mrs Parkes, who had been told of their son's behaviour, were setting out with all speed to try to find him; Verity, Celia, and their parents were to depart that day as well; which only left Squire Walters and his family, and the squire showed no signs of being dislodged.

And then Miss Trumble, after she had waved goodbye to the farmer and his cross sister, saw the little Beverley carriage coming up the drive.

Barry had returned.

She waited while he drove up. 'How goes it, Barry?' she asked. 'I have missed your company and your good sense.' She turned to a waiting groom. 'Be so good as to take Mr Wort's carriage to the stables.' She turned to Barry. 'Come indoors and we shall have a comfortable coze.'

'You make me feel like a gentleman,' said Barry with a grin. 'You should have seen that groom's face – being ordered to attend to a mere servant's carriage.'

'I confess I am rather weary of social ranks after this morning,' said Miss Trumble as they walked indoors and up the stairs. 'We will go to my private sitting-room, where we will not be disturbed. I have so much to tell you.'

She waited until they were comfortably ensconced and then asked, 'And how goes Lady Beverley?'

'My lady is quite animated,' said Barry. 'If I may be so bold as to say so, miss, she is toadied to quite dreadfully by Mrs Judd and it appears to have raised her spirits wonderfully. My lady was quite happy to have me act as footman, but she became friendly with a certain Mrs Handley who asked her why I was so oddly shaped for a footman, not being tall or slim, and my lady became ashamed of me and ordered me home.'

'And glad I am that you are here again,' said Miss Trumble.

She told him everything that had happened.

'Do you think that the engagement will really be broken after a few months?' asked Barry when she had finished.

'I do not know, Barry,' said Miss Trumble on a sigh. 'They are acting as if they are fond of each other. But the difference in age and temperament is great.'

'Her sisters all married men older than they,' Barry pointed out.

'I do not know Gervase very well,' said Miss

Trumble. 'Lizzie is so young and passionate and Gervase appears a cold fish by comparison.'

'Is my lady to be told of the deception?'

'Lady Beverley? No. She will make such a scene. Sufficient unto the day is the evil thereof.'

Lizzie dressed with great care, wondering all the time what her mother's reaction to the announcement of her engagement would be. She felt like a fraud and was weary of this charade of an engagement. She would tell the duke to let her end it as soon as possible and then she would go and stay with one of her sisters, but shuddered at the idea of a Season. So much expense just to find a suitable mate! Better to remain single like Miss Trumble. But Miss Trumble was not Miss Trumble but the duke's aunt and surely could not work as a governess for much longer.

At least I am not plotting to really marry him to get Mannerling, thought Lizzie. I hate this place now. It warps people's minds and brings nothing but misery. It is a pity that I and the duke do not really suit, for Mannerling is simply another residence to him.

She suddenly shivered. She could feel menace surrounding her, an air of malignant threat. The house is plotting something, she thought. Mannerling will never leave us in peace.

Squire Walters was feeling exhausted and was settling down to enjoy a bottle of the duke's best port to reward himself. He had shouted at his daughter, but to little effect. Sarah had retreated into a really splendid dream. Lizzie Beverley was dying of consumption. She, Sarah, had nursed her rival faithfully, but Lizzie was about to expire. Sarah and the duke faced each other across Lizzie's recumbent body. 'I do not know how to thank you for your selfless devotion to my fiancée,' said the duke, staring at her with burning eyes. 'My darling, you must be exhausted.'

'You must not call me that!' exclaimed dream Sarah.

'I cannot stop myself. I have grown to love you.' And so on. And somewhere outside this dream, her father's nagging, berating voice was simply an irritating buzz, like a summer fly trapped against a window pane.

The squire had then slapped and punched his wife, saying it was all her fault they had such a widgeon for a daughter. Mrs Walters had curled herself up into a ball like a hedgehog and prayed for his death.

He had left her weeping and settled down to enjoy the port.

He had drunk almost the whole bottle and his wife's irritating weeping from the next room had stopped at last when he heard his name called from a distance. 'Squire Walters!'

It was a light, silvery voice and yet a compelling voice.

He got to his feet and went to the door and opened it.

There it was again, echoing faintly in the corridor. 'Squire Walters'.

The port had been rich and heavy. He staggered slightly and clung on to the door jamb. But the voice called again, more insistent this time.

He walked out into the corridor. The drunkenness seemed to leave him and he felt quite young and light.

He moved towards the sound of that voice until he found himself on the landing, overlooking the Great Hall.

'Squire Walters! Squire Walters! Look down!' The voice held a mocking edge now.

He leaned over the balustrade.

'I am here – underneath, waiting for you,' challenged the voice. 'Look down! Look down!'

And then drunkenness closed around him like a black cloud. He felt dizzy and faint. He clutched tightly on to the mahogany rail of the balustrade. It seemed to melt under his hands. He let out a great scream of fear.

A servant crossing the hall cried out as the body of the squire hurtled down, hit the tiles with a sickening thud and lay still.

One by one the servants crept into the hall and formed a circle around the dead man. A thin trickle of blood began to flow from his head across the tiles.

'What's amiss?'

The duke's voice sounded down into the hall.

A footman found his voice. 'It's the squire, Your Grace. He's dead.'

The duke ran down the stairs and the servants parted to let him through. He felt the squire's pulse. There was a faint flicker of life. 'Get the physician,' he shouted. 'He's not dead yet.'

The squire's lips were moving. The duke knelt down on the floor beside him.

'The voice was calling me,' said the squire in a

faint whisper. 'The banister melted under my hands.'

'Try not to speak,' urged the duke. 'Help will be here shortly.'

'Too late,' came the weak whisper. Then there was a rattle in the back of the squire's throat. The duke felt his pulse again but there was no life at all. 'He's dead now.' The duke rose and then looked up.

Lizzie was standing on the landing, looking down. Her face was paper-white. The duke ran up the stairs again and gathered her shaking body in his arms.

'Do not be afraid,' he said, kissing her hair. 'Come away. There is nothing you can do.'

'Was it the house that killed him?' asked Lizzie, but her face was pressed against his chest and he did not hear her.

Miss Trumble, later that day, entered Mrs Walters's room. The widow sat motionless in a chair staring at the empty fireplace.

Miss Trumble quietly sat down. Neither woman spoke until Mrs Walters said quietly, 'I will go to hell.'

'I doubt that very much, my dear,' said Miss Trumble. 'What great crime have you committed that you should be punished so?'

'It is all my fault,' said Mrs Walters.

'You did not push him to his death. The servant who saw him fall said he was alone on the landing.'

'I prayed that he would die,' said Mrs Walters in a harsh whisper.

Miss Trumble leaned forward and took her hand in a firm grip. 'If God killed all the people we wished dead, then the world would be a poorly populated place. Did he bully you?'

'He beat me. He beat me this morning.'

'Will you be comfortably off now he is dead?'

'Yes; because we have no son, everything comes to me.'

Miss Trumble pressed her hand harder. 'When the fright and shock and guilt have all gone, you will slowly begin to appreciate your new circumstances. You will rise of a morning and give the day's commands to the servants with no one to countermand your instructions, you will be able to read novels and go for walks. You will be able to entertain friends. And perhaps your daughter, Sarah, will not need to hide out in dreams. Think about it, and gather your courage.'

Sarah Walters was sitting in her room, her face suffused with the glow of love. For the duke had called on her to offer his sympathies. She had thrown herself at him, crying and saying she had been a bad daughter, and he had spoken soothing words to her before putting her from him.

She played that affecting scene over and over in her mind. The duke had been trying to tell her it was she he loved. He must be released from this engagement. Something would need to happen to Lizzie.

Her brain was now quite turned by her father's death. Sarah was deeply involved in her fantasy world.

The banisters on the landing were low. One

quick push and all would believe that Lizzie, too, had become dizzy and fallen to her death. But she would need to act quickly. Arrangements were already being made for her father's body to be taken home, and she and her mother with it. The duke was offering his outriders and footmen to augment their own servants – a sign of love and affection if there ever was one! They were to leave the following day. But her great love for the duke would make things happen as they were meant to happen. She felt all-powerful.

Miss Trumble had persuaded the duke to allow Barry to stay. She felt uneasy, and longed for the moment when she could wave goodbye to Mrs Walters and Sarah. The duke and Lizzie had dropped any pretence of being fond of each other and were politely formal, but Miss Trumble knew that both were still shocked over the death of the squire. She had hoped the tragedy would bring them closer together, but instead it seemed to have driven them apart.

Lizzie had been hurt that the duke had not found it necessary to ask her how she was coping with the terrible shock of seeing the dead squire and had decided that the engagement was, after all, in name only. Mannerling was a house of mourning. The squire's body had been laid out, a coffin was being brought from Hedgefield that day in which he would be conveyed home, and that dead figure seemed etched on her brain. She had gone to pay her respects to the dead man.

He had been lying still and small in death, candles at either side of the bed. Mrs Walters had been kneeling, praying, and Sarah had been sitting on a chair in the room, an odd little smile on her lips which unnerved Lizzie more than the dead squire.

She collected a gown which had a torn hem, along with her work-basket, and went along to the drawing-room. Tiffin, radiant with happiness, rose to meet her.

'How goes Miss Walters?'

'I do not quite know,' said Lizzie with a sigh. 'She looks quite odd but that is to be expected. It was a most strange accident.'

'Peter said he smelt most strongly of drink and the banister on the landing is quite low.'

'Have you seen our host?'

'I overheard one of the servants say he had gone riding.'

He might have offered to take me with him, thought Lizzie moodily. It would be wonderful to ride away from this house of death.

Peter Bond came in. Tiffin blushed and curtsied. He murmured something to her and then said, 'Excuse us,' and led Tiffin from the room.

And that is how it should be, thought Lizzie. But the thought of the duke smiling at *her* dotingly made her laugh. She opened her work-basket, took out needle and thread, and bent her head over the torn flounce in the gown on her lap.

The duke entered quietly and stood for a moment surveying her. Lizzie looked up and saw him. 'Do not trouble to rise.' He walked forward and sat down opposite her. He was wearing riding dress. He stretched out his booted legs. 'The announcement of our engagement is in the news-papers this morning,' he said.

Lizzie coloured. 'It will be the first intelligence Mama has of it.'

'You did not write to her immediately?'

'With everything that is going on here, I forgot.'

'Then I assume Lady Beverley will be soon heading in this direction with all speed.'

'I am afraid so,' said Lizzie. 'Mama will be in alt. I only hope she does not suffer a bad *crise de nerfs* when she learns it is all a sham. Should we not tell her as soon as she arrives and get it over with?'

'I consulted my aunt on the matter. She urged me to leave matters as they are for the moment.'

'Oh, well,' said Lizzie, putting a neat stitch in the flounce, 'I suppose we will just have to look as if we like each other.'

'As to that, I was under the impression that we did like each other.'

'I do not know you very well, Your Grace.'

'Gervase.'

'Gervase, then.'

'What is it about me you do not know?'

Lizzie looked at him impatiently. 'When I am with you I feel I am facing some sort of employer.'

'In a way you are. You are being used by me to keep up the pretence of an engagement. Is that so very difficult?'

'Not at the moment. But it will be after Mama arrives. She will assume ... airs.'

'I am not marrying her, my sweeting.'

'You are not marrying me either, Gervase.'

'True. But when I am with you, I seem to forget

that fact.'

She looked up at him sharply, but his eyes were amused.

The door opened and Sarah Walters came in.

The duke was sitting on a sofa facing Lizzie. Sarah sat down beside him and took his hand and gazed into his eyes. 'I can never thank you enough for your kindness to me,' she breathed.

He drew his hand away. 'You are welcome, Miss Walters. And now if you will excuse me...?'

Lizzie sent him a fulminating glare, but he only smiled, rose and bowed to both of them and left the room.

There was an awkward silence. Lizzie was embarrassed because she felt Sarah looked odder than ever. Her eyes were blazing in her white face.

'I feel like taking the air, Miss Beverley,' she said.

'Do you wish me to get a footman to accompany you?' asked Lizzie.

'Oh, do not trouble.' Sarah tittered. 'You are not yet a duchess and can hardly order his servants around. I would appreciate your company.'

'Alas, I am busy mending this flounce.'

'Will no one have any sympathy for me?' cried Sarah. 'Is it too much to ask? I crave some fresh air.'

'Very well,' said Lizzie, relenting. 'I will fetch my bonnet and shawl.'

'Thank you,' said Sarah. 'I will meet you on the landing.'

Lizzie went to her room and tied on a bonnet and put a warm shawl about her shoulders, for the day was blustery.

Sarah must be slightly deranged, poor girl, thought Lizzie, to even think of meeting anyone on that cursed landing.

She made her way to the landing. To her surprise, Sarah was standing there, but still dressed only in a black gown. No bonnet or shawl.

'You have not yet changed,' said Lizzie.

'No matter.' Sarah's eyes burned with a feverish light. 'Come here, Miss Beverley. It was here he fell.'

Lizzie joined her and put a hand on her arm. 'Come away,' she said gently. 'You must put it behind you. Come away.'

Sarah leaned over the low balustrade. 'Do come away from there!' cried Lizzie sharply.

'There is someone lying down there,' exclaimed Sarah.

'I am sure there is no one,' said Lizzie soothingly.

'But look! Only look! Down there!'

Lizzie leaned over.

Sarah gave her a tremendous push. Lizzie saw the tiles of the floor seeming to race up towards her but she had been clutching the balustrade tightly. She flung herself backwards.

'Die!' screamed Sarah, grabbing her by the shoulders and pushing her back to the balustrade. 'He really loves me. Not you! Me!'

'What is going on here?'

Sarah released Lizzie and turned, panting. The duke stood there. Sarah flung herself into his arms. 'She tried to kill me,' she said. 'Lizzie tried to push me over. She knows we are in love, Gervase, and so she tried to kill me.'

167

Two footmen had come racing up the stairs. The duke pried Sarah's clutching arms from around his neck.

'Take Miss Walters to her room,' he commanded, 'and lock her in and post yourselves on guard at the door.' He put an arm around Lizzie's shoulders. 'Come with me.'

The footmen seized Sarah and bore her off. Her wild screams echoed back to their ears.

Lizzie was shaking all over. She let him guide her back to the drawing-room. He pushed her into a chair and then knelt in front of her. He untied the strings of her bonnet and took off her hat. Then he rubbed her cold hands. 'What happened?'

In a broken voice, Lizzie told him.

'There, now. It is over and they will soon be gone. That servant of yours, Barry, is here. I will send for him and he will guard you until the Walters have left. Wait and I will fetch him.'

She caught one of his hands. 'Do not leave me, Gervase.'

'Only as far as the bell-rope.'

But at that moment not only Barry but Miss Trumble entered the room. The duke told them what had happened and gave Barry his orders.

'And where is Miss Walters now?' asked Miss Trumble.

'In her room, under guard.'

'I shall go and see her. Barry, take Lizzie to her room and stay with her. I tell you, Gervase, you should sell this place, quit this place. It is evil.'

'At this moment, I think it is Miss Walters that is evil,' said the duke. 'Go to her by all means,

168

Aunt, and ascertain that she is safe to travel or if she should be confined in the nearest bedlam.'

Miss Trumble went along to Sarah's room. One of the footmen unlocked the door for her. Miss Trumble went in. The room was in darkness. Sarah's white face glared at her out of the gloom.

Miss Trumble went over to the window, opened the curtains, threw open the shutters and then opened the window. Sunlight flooded the room and the curtains streamed out in the wind.

'I am letting in some sanity,' said Miss Trumble, turning around. 'If you have any wits left, can you bring yourself to tell me why you tried to kill Miss Beverley?'

The hectic light had left Sarah's eyes. 'She tried to kill *me*,' she said sullenly.

'We both know that is not true.'

'He does not love her!'

'The duke most certainly does not love you, Sarah Walters.'

She hung her head. Then she said, 'Will I be arrested?'

'As you richly deserve to be? No, it would make a tiresome scandal and your poor mother has suffered enough. Have you no concern for her?'

Sarah stared at the floor.

'I think you live in dreams and fantasies that have nothing to do with the real world,' said Miss Trumble.

'You are right,' said Sarah heavily. 'I will make Mr Bond happy. He truly loves me and he will have his reward.'

'Grant me patience!' cried the exasperated governess. 'Mr Bond is engaged to be married to

Miss Moon.'

'She stole him from me.'

'Fustian! He fell in love with a pretty girl, and if you had not been so wrapped up in your mad dreams, you might have noticed he has as little interest in you as the duke.'

Sarah began to cry.

Miss Trumble watched her coldly. 'I have no sympathy for you, Sarah. I wish from the bottom of my heart that you were crying not for yourself and the wreck of your silly dreams, but for your father. You will be kept here until the morning, when we will all be glad to see the last of you.'

Miss Trumble left. The key clicked in the door. Sarah searched her mind desperately for a dream but none would come.

SEVEN

Youth will be served, every dog has his day, and mine has been a fine one.

GEORGE BORROW

Miss Trumble watched from her window the following day as the Walters' carriage moved slowly down the long drive flanked by outriders, and followed by another carriage draped in black, which contained the squire's body.

She wondered what Sarah was dreaming about now.

But inside the carriage, Sarah was dreamless.

As the carriage swept through the gates of Mannerling, she could feel all the events of her visit moving away from her as they moved away, for the house, now seen in retrospect, seemed like some mad and evil dream.

She leaned forward and took her mother's hand. 'I am truly sorry,' said Sarah.

'We will support each other now, my child,' said Mrs Walters. 'We are going home.'

'We will be safe there,' said Sarah. 'I think I was very insane, Mama.'

'We will talk about it later,' said Mrs Walters. She tried to think sad thoughts about her dead husband, but as the distance grew between them and Mannerling, she could only think of how pleasant her future would be now.

Lady Beverley and Mary Judd strolled together in the Pump Room at Bath – well, not *quite* together, for Mary had taken to walking just a little behind in a respectful way, a little courtesy which had moved Lady Beverley to buying Mary a new silk gown and bonnet. Mary had given up wearing black and thought that the shade of her gown, a delicate lilac, was very becoming, as was her new straw hat with the brim lined in pleated lilac silk.

Lady Beverley saw old Lady Parton approaching and stiffened. Lady Parton was a baroness, a great gossip, and a great snob. She had even dared to act coldly and grandly to Lady Beverley.

But for once Lady Parton's round face was wreathed in smiles. 'Dear Lady Beverley,' she cried, 'you must be in heaven this morning.'

'I am not in heaven or anywhere else but the Pump Room in Bath,' declared Lady Beverley. 'Do adjust my shawl, Mary. It is slipping a trifle.'

'But your news, such wonderful news,' exclaimed Lady Parton. 'Such a triumph for your youngest.'

'Lizzie? What of Lizzie?'

'Lady Beverley, have you not seen the announcement in the newspapers this morning?'

'I have not yet seen the newspapers.'

'Then I bring you good tidings. Your daughter, Lizzie, is engaged to Severnshire.'

Lady Beverley stared at Lady Parton for a long moment. 'Ah, yes,' she said, rallying. 'I knew about that. Come along, Mary.'

With Mary dutifully following, Lady Beverley walked on. Then she put out a hand to lean on a pillar as if to steady herself. 'What is this?' she whispered savagely to Mary. 'Lizzie to be married to Severnshire? Can it be true? Why was I not informed?'

'I have always thought your daughters a trifle unfeeling,' said Mary, who had done a lot of work during this visit to Bath to pour poison about the Beverley sisters into their mother's usually discontented ears, for Mary hoped that Lady Beverley would change her will in her, Mary's, favour.

'Curb your tongue, miss,' snapped Lady Beverley. 'We must return. We must get a newspaper. Goodness me, I feel quite faint. Lizzie! Lizzie, of all people. I always said she had a rare beauty.'

Mary forbore from mentioning that day in and day out Lady Beverley had complained of Lizzie's pert tongue and lack of looks.

They hurried up the steep hills of Bath from the Pump Room to the Royal Crescent, Lady Beverley showing quite amazing energy for such a perpetual invalid, while Mary struggled to keep up.

They hurried to the drawing-room of Lady Beverley's rented house, where the morning papers were laid out on a console table, as yet unread.

Lady Beverley seized *The Morning Post* and rustled it open and turned to the social page. And there was the announcement. She stared at it.

She sat down suddenly. 'I cannot understand it. When could this have happened, Mary? And why did my unfeeling daughter leave me to find out such momentous news in this way?'

Mary's black eyes sparkled with curiosity. 'I would humbly suggest, my lady, that we return with all speed.'

'Yes, yes, we must do that. Tell the servants to pack. Let me see. Tell the agent we will be quitting this house immediately and I expect a month's rent to be returned to me. And the servants will need to be paid off. We have no time to wait for Barry. And hire a post-chaise.'

In that moment, Mary felt she had borne enough. She was tired of being treated like a servant. After all, she, too, had lived at Mannerling.

Mannerling!

The angry words died unsaid on Mary's lips. 'Lizzie will have Mannerling,' she said slowly. 'You will be going home.'

Lady Beverley's pale eyes began to burn with a

173

fierce light. 'Yes, Mannerling. Oh, my dear Mary, home at last!'

'Of course,' said Mary, 'I had quite forgot.'

'Forgot what?'

'That Mannerling is not the duke's main residence. He will return to his palace in Severnshire and may sell Mannerling.'

Lady Beverley stiffened. 'Over my dead body. Oh, we must leave immediately. Lizzie is not to be trusted. She must make him keep the place. Don't stand there. See to the arrangements.'

Mary sat down. 'I am feeling a trifle fatigued,' she said. 'I would suggest, my lady, that you command the servants to see to the arrangements.'

'But they are silly people. Come, Mary, this is not like you.'

'I resent being treated like a servant.' Mary had suddenly decided that because of Lizzie's great coup, there was no hope of getting any of Lady Beverley's money.

Lady Beverley thought quickly. She had become used to Mary's toadying. And now that her daughter was to marry a duke, she could afford to be generous. She found it hard to give up her usual miserly ways, but she wanted to depart as quickly as possible and Mary was capable of arranging everything for their departure efficiently.

'Do you remember that you always admired my gold-and-ruby necklace?' she said cajolingly.

Mary's little black eyes lit up. Lady Beverley had begun to open the purse strings since she had come to Bath and had bought herself that necklace from Bath's finest jeweller.

'I admire it very much,' breathed Mary.

174

'Then it is yours. Now, my dear friend, what about the travel arrangements?'

Mary smiled. 'You are kindness itself, my lady. I will set about our preparations to go home.'

When they finally arrived at Brookfield House, they received the startling intelligence that Miss Trumble and Lizzie were both resident at Mannerling and had been since the day Lady Beverley and Mary had left.

'On to Mannerling,' Lady Beverley commanded the driver.

'How odd,' said Mary as the carriage lurched on the road to Mannerling. 'They left for Mannerling the same day that we left for Bath. Therefore, before we left, they already knew they were going.'

'I cannot understand it,' said Lady Beverley. 'That scheming governess is behind this.'

'I do not know how you tolerate that woman,' said Mary. 'You must dismiss her.'

'I cannot dismiss the duke's aunt until she chooses to go.'

'His aunt!'

'I am afraid I have let the secret out. Miss Trumble is actually Lady Letitia Revine.'

'But why should such a great lady stoop to be a mere governess?'

'I have thought of that. She is eccentric and was moved to take the job because of our high standing.'

'Or perhaps,' said Mary with a titter, 'there is a black scandal in her past. Only think if that were the case! Think of the peril your daughters have been in.'

'Lady Letitia said she would remain until Lizzie was wed. But you must address her as Miss Trumble. It is supposed to be a secret.'

Mary turned this news over in her busy mind, wondering if there might be some way she could turn it to her advantage.

'Home!' exclaimed Lady Beverley as the lodge-keeper swung open the great iron gates of Mannerling.

'Home,' echoed Mary.

Unaware that the lady who now regarded herself as his future mother-in-law was about to descend on him, the duke was searching for Lizzie. She had been avoiding him, he was sure of that, and it had begun to annoy him. The evening before, she had sent down word that she would not be joining him for dinner but would eat something on a tray in her room as she was feeling 'poorly'. Although most of his mind had not believed her, there was still a niggling little part of it that had feared she might be really ill. But when he had called at her rooms that morning, it was to find her absent and that his aunt was not available to consult, for his servants told him she had gone out riding with Barry. That had infuriated him as well, for he considered his aunt's friendship with this low servant quite unsuitable.

He strode out of the house. And then he heard the sounds of laughter. They were coming from the side of the house, coming faintly to his ears on the summer air.

He strode off in the direction from which the laughter was coming. He found them in the west lawn, Lizzie, Peter and Tiffin, playing at skittles. Lizzie was laughing, her hair tumbled out of its pins, Peter was in his shirtsleeves, and Tiffin was applauding their performance.

And then they saw him. Tiffin looked scared, Peter ran to put on his jacket and then stood to attention, and Lizzie swept her red hair up and pinned it back in place. That all made him like some elderly, overbearing parent.

'I was just about to go about my duties, Your Grace,' said Peter, and hurried off. Tiffin curtsied, murmured something and then scampered off after him. Lizzie and the duke faced each other.

'I am glad to see you restored to health,' said the duke.

'Yes, it was only a headache. Now, if you will excuse me, Gervase ... I must go and find Miss Trumble.'

'My aunt has gone out with that servant, Barry.'

'Oh.' She stood irresolute and he guessed she was trying to find another excuse to leave him.

'You are not playing your part very well, Lizzie.'

'As your betrothed? But there is no one here to act for.'

'We used to converse at least. Why do you avoid me now?'

'I find my situation awkward,' said Lizzie slowly. 'I do not know quite how to go on.'

'We could go on as friends.'

Lizzie looked at him doubtfully.

'Why do you look at me so?'

'I have often wondered why you wear your hair in such an old-fashioned style, tied back with a ribbon.'

'Do you wish me to cut it?'

'No, no, Gervase. My wishes are nothing to you.'

'Do you think it makes me look too old?'

Lizzie blushed. His hair was very thick and as glossy as her own. She had just had a treacherous little dream where she was burying her hands in his thick hair.

'I see you think it does.'

'Oh, no,' said Lizzie miserably. 'I think your hair is very fine.'

'I hear carriage wheels,' he said.

'That will probably be Mama.' Lizzie bit her lip. 'I suppose we must go on with our masquerade. And yet, is it really necessary? I mean, it is not fashionable to be in love.'

He took her hand and raised it to his lips. Then he began to lead her back towards the front of the house. 'For your mother's temporary peace of mind, I think we should try to show some affection towards each other.'

He tucked her hand in his arm. I cannot bear much more of this, thought Lizzie. I want him to really love me. I am frightened of betraying myself.

'Yes,' he said, as they reached the front of the house. 'Your mother is arrived.'

They stood together as the post-chaise swept up to the front door.

For once in her life, Lady Beverley did not wait for the footman to let down the steps. She hurtled out of the carriage and spread her arms wide.

'Home at last!' she cried.

Lizzie stepped forward and kissed her mother

on the cheek. How could her mother think that, even supposing they were to be married, the duke would live at Mannerling?

She glanced at the duke and saw the look of weary distaste on his face, quickly masked.

'You are welcome to stay as my guest, Lady Beverley,' said the duke heavily. 'But no doubt you will be more comfortable in your own home.'

'But this *is* my home,' cried Lady Beverley. 'And may I present Mrs Judd? She will be staying as well.'

'Pray come in,' said the duke, 'and I will inform the housekeeper of your arrival. Ah, Mr Bond. Lady Beverley and Mrs Judd will be residing with us. Arrange rooms for them, if you please.'

Peter bowed.

The duke turned to Lizzie. 'Come with me, dearest,' he said. 'We have much to discuss.'

Lizzie followed him up the staircase, feeling smaller and more diminished with every step. Once more, she felt she was the plain Beverley sister. Already she was dreading the scenes and recriminations when her mother found out the truth.

The duke led her into the drawing-room and then turned to face her.

'I have been neglecting my estates, Lizzie, and it is time I returned to attend to matters at my home.'

'Will you not stay a few days until Mama is settled?'

'I have already endured a dreadful house party and the death of Squire Walters. I do not want to endure another stressful time.'

'Do you wish me to accompany you, Gervase?' she asked in a small voice.

'No, I will leave you here with your mother.'

Lizzie looked at him, her eyes sparkling with tears. 'It is all so humiliating.'

'But you know our engagement to be only a temporary arrangement.'

'It is not that,' said Lizzie wretchedly. 'It is your great pride. You have met Mama again and you already feel distaste for even being involved in a temporary arrangement.'

'True,' he said. 'But we will cope.'

'How long will you be away?'

'I do not know. Several weeks.'

'And you would leave me here ... in this house?'

'You lived here before.'

'And there has been nothing but death and misery here ever since.'

'Then you should all go to Brookfield House and await my return.'

'Mama will not be dislodged unless we tell her the truth.'

'As to that, it is for you to decide what you tell her and when you tell her. I do not know how you came by such an unnatural parent, Lizzie.'

'You should not criticize my mother so!'

'My apologies. I shall leave Mr Bond behind. You may apply to him for anything you wish.'

'When do you leave?'

'Tomorrow.'

She stood before him, silent.

'You will be able to enjoy yourself with your young friends when I am gone,' he said, 'and my aunt will stand between you and your mother

180

and that odd creature who accompanies her.'

Lizzie curtsied. 'I wish you a safe journey, Your Grace.'

'Ah, Lizzie,' he said, stretching out a hand. 'We could deal better than this.'

But there was a roaring in her ears and she did not hear him. She opened the door of the drawing-room and went out. She was dimly aware through her tears of a dark figure fleeing along the corridor in front of her but was too distressed to wonder who it was.

Mary Judd stopped a passing maid and demanded to be shown to her room. Her heart was beating hard. Instead of following Lady Beverley, she had hidden behind a curtain in a window embrasure until she had heard the duke and Lizzie going into the drawing-room. Then she had left her hiding place and pressed her ear against the panels of the door.

What she had heard had amazed her and then infuriated her. Mary always listened at doors because she was convinced that everyone must be discussing what an interesting and fascinating lady she was, and although that had never happened, she lived in hope.

She was stunned by what she had heard. For some reason, the engagement was a pretence and she had heard herself dismissed as an odd creature. Her revenge against the haughty Beverleys when she had married Judd and moved in as mistress of Mannerling had been of short duration only.

Now she had the means to revenge herself on

Lady Beverley for all the humiliations of Bath.

She decided that the duke's reference to an odd creature must have applied to the maid, Betty. The duke would hardly refer to a lady such as herself in such terms. Her amour propre restored and looking forward immensely to telling Lady Beverley her great news, she removed her hat and gloves and mantle, smoothed down her hair, smiled at her reflection in the mirror, and rang the bell.

From the maid who answered the bell, she found out that Lady Beverley was quartered in rooms next to her own and went and opened that lady's door and went in.

Lady Beverley was sitting at the toilet-table applying cream to her face.

'I feel young again, Mary,' said Lady Beverley. 'Mannerling will be restored to its former glory. I am sure the duke's taste cannot match my own. You will remember, Mary, my taste was the talk of the county. Dear Lizzie. She was always my favourite.'

Mary sat down behind Lady Beverley where she could clearly see their reflections in the mirror. She did not want to miss any reaction to her momentous news.

'I was passing the drawing-room, my lady,' said Mary in her customary meek voice. 'The door was standing open and I heard the duke and Lizzie talking. I would not have listened but what they were saying shocked me immensely.'

'Ah, then, Mary,' said Lady Beverley with a little laugh, 'you should not listen to the conversation of lovers and you will not be shocked.'

'They're not lovers. In fact, they are not really engaged,' said Mary. 'They said it was only a temporary arrangement. The duke leaves for his estates tomorrow. He said to Lizzie he did not know how she had come by such an unnatural parent. Lizzie said he was ashamed of even a temporary engagement because of you, my lady.'

Lady Beverley's face turned white under her cream. 'You must have misheard,' she panted. 'You are a wicked, wicked woman! A temporary engagement! Why, all that means is that they plan to be married very soon. Go away, Mary, I will have none of your spite.'

'It is not spite, my lady,' said Mary. 'Have I not cared for you, been your friend, appreciated your qualities when your own family did not? If you do not believe me, then you have only to ask them.'

Lady Beverley carefully wiped the cream from her face and applied powder. Then she rose to her feet. 'Wait here, you,' she said haughtily. 'I will deal with you later.'

The duke was pacing the drawing-room in a fever of indecision. He had made Lizzie cry and now he was abandoning her. But she had made it so plain that she did not relish his company that he had felt he was doing the right thing in leaving her, and yes, she had been right. He had felt he could not bear to be under the same roof as her mother.

He felt rejected by Lizzie. That damned reflection of himself as an old man would not leave him.

He turned as the door opened and Lady

Beverley swept in.

'Lady Beverley?'

'My silly companion has come to me with an odd story. She says she overheard you tell my Lizzie that the engagement was only a temporary one.'

He looked at her wearily. 'Am I always to be plagued with interfering malicious people? May I point out that my conversation with your daughter was private? The drawing-room doors were closed.'

'Nonetheless, what did you mean by it?'

He felt the need of support. He rang the bell. 'Sit down, Lady Beverley.'

When the butler came in, he said, 'Is Miss Trumble returned?'

'Yes, Your Grace.'

'Ask her to join us, and Miss Beverley as well.'

'But I must know,' wailed Lady Beverley.

'Wait!'

After a short time, Miss Trumble came in with Lizzie.

'What is this?' demanded Lady Beverley, before the duke could speak. 'Is it only a temporary engagement? And what does a temporary engagement mean?'

'I will explain,' said Miss Trumble. 'His Grace took Lizzie riding to Hedgefield. They wished some refreshment and so he engaged a private parlour at the Green Man. To allay scandal, it was agreed that there should be an engagement for a few months, after which time Lizzie would terminate it.'

'No, that will never do,' said Lady Beverley.

'It has been done, Mama,' said Lizzie impatiently. 'The announcement has appeared in the newspapers.'

'Yes, and came as a surprise to me. My own daughter not to even trouble to write to me! But of course you must be married, Lizzie.'

'Perhaps eventually,' said Lizzie drily.

'I mean to Severnshire here.'

Lizzie stared at her mother. 'But it has been explained to you how the engagement came about and why it must be over shortly.'

'No, no, child. You do not understand, and you, too, Miss Trumble, should have known better. It is quite likely that Lizzie will not marry. Therefore the scandal about her meeting with the duke will go on and everyone will say he rejected *her*. People do not reject dukes.'

'We do not all hold such a low opinion of your daughter as you evidently entertain, Lady Beverley,' said the duke furiously.

'I am sick of this,' shouted Lizzie. 'I am sick of Mannerling. I am sick of the Beverley ambition. I do not want to marry the duke. There! Let that be an end of it.'

Lady Beverley went into strong hysterics and Mary Judd trotted into the room and solicitously took her away.

'I am sorry, Gervase,' said Miss Trumble, 'but you must see that Lizzie was excessively provoked.'

'As was I,' said the duke coldly. 'I have no intention of allying my name with such a family. Mr Bond, make sure Lady Beverley and that creature with her are gone on my return.'

185

He, too, marched from the room. Miss Trumble felt close to tears. She felt she should go to Lizzie, but there was nothing she could do. It was all too clear that Lizzie did not want to marry the duke.

As if to suit the dark mood enveloping the house, the day clouded over and thunder began to rumble in the distance.

Only Miss Trumble and the duke sat down to dinner that evening. Lady Beverley was keeping to her room, attended by Mary Judd, Tiffin had taken Peter to visit her father, and Lizzie had sent down a curt note of apology.

'Do you wish to talk to me about your relationship with Lizzie?' ventured Miss Trumble at last.

'No,' he said curtly. 'We have no relationship, so there is nothing to talk about.'

'Then why are you so angry?'

'May I say that a visit from Lady Beverley is enough to freeze anyone up?'

'And there is nothing else? You have no feeling for Lizzie?'

'None.'

They finished their meal in silence.

Thunder crashed and roared above Mannerling as Lizzie wearily sat down in front of the mirror to take out her pins and prepare herself for bed. Two branches of candles on the marble toilet-table lit her wan face.

Then, as she looked at the mirror, she let out a gasp. She was attending a wedding. She was sitting in the balcony at St George's, Hanover Square. Below her the duke was marrying a figure in white. The figure turned round and smiled up at the duke. It was Lady Verity. And then Lizzie realized that sitting next to her were Mr Judd, Harry Devers, Mr Cater, Perry Vane and Squire Walters, their white leering faces staring at her malignantly. Mr Judd had committed suicide, Harry Devers had leaped to his death from a London roof, pursued by the Runners, Perry Vane, cousin of a previous owner, Lord St Clair, had been burnt to death and Squire Walters had fallen to his death in the Great Hall of Mannerling.

'No!' screamed Lizzie. The image faded and she was once more staring at her own face.

She rose to her feet. Gervase must not marry Verity. She could not bear it. Perhaps the mirror had tricked her eyes, but it could be some sort of warning.

She knew the duke's rooms were her father's old ones, and picking up her bed-candle, she hurried along the corridors, which were lit by bright flashes of lightning.

She scratched at the door of the duke's bed-chamber, but the crashes of thunder were so loud that she was sure he could not hear her. She pushed open the door and went in.

The duke was lying in a bath in front of the fire.

'Lizzie,' he exclaimed. 'What is the matter?'

Lizzie approached the bath, her eyes averted. 'That mirror in my room, the one that used to be here, I saw your wedding in it.'

'And whom was I marrying? You?'

'No, Lady Verity, and I cannot bear it.'

'Come here.'

She sidled up to the bath, her eyes still averted. He reached out a hand and pulled her towards him. 'You are not respectable, Gervase!' cried Lizzie.

'All your complaints have been that I am too respectable and stuffy by half. I also think I have been blind and stupid.'

He gave one more savage tug and she toppled over into the bath on top of him. He caught her face and bent his mouth to hers and began to kiss her long and passionately while she trembled against his naked body, until she stopped trembling and returned kiss for kiss.

'Why did you tell me you didn't want me?' he murmured at last, against her mouth.

'I wanted you to love me,' whispered Lizzie against his wet chest. 'I did not want to be friends.'

'So you will let me make a respectable lady of you?'

She raised her face. 'Oh yes, please, Gervase.'

'So kiss me again.'

Miss Trumble quietly opened the door ten minutes later and then shut it again and sped back along the corridor to the safety of her room.

She slammed the door behind her and leaned against it, gasping a little with shock. The sight that had met her eyes in the duke's room was not the sort of thing any respectable spinster should ever see.

She should go back along there and lecture them on such disgusting and wanton behaviour. Her elderly face broke into a puckish grin.

On the other hand, she could thank God and go to bed and mind her own business.

And that is exactly what she did.

EPILOGUE

I expect that Woman will be the last thing civilized by Man.

GEORGE MEREDITH

Ten years had passed since the wedding of Lizzie Beverley to the Duke of Severnshire. Lady Beverley and Mary Judd were resident at Mannerling. The duke had given them permission to live there for as long as Lady Beverley lived.

Lizzie was now the proud mother of four children, three boys and one girl. The girl, Isabella, was nine years old and had her mother's elfin looks and green eyes. Lizzie, the duke and their children were just completing their first visit to Mannerling since their wedding, both Lizzie and the duke having previously refused to return there, and saying that if Lady Beverley wanted to see them, then she should travel to the duke's palace.

Lizzie had been nervous at the thought of returning, but the house now seemed just a house and she found it hard to believe she had ever imagined it to be haunted. A magnificent crystal chandelier now hung once more in the Great Hall of Mannerling, but it did not swing or tinkle when there was no wind. The ghosts, thought Lizzie, if there had ever been any, had been laid to rest.

'I only wish your aunt could have been here with us,' sighed Lizzie, joining him in his room before their departure.

'I think Aunt Letitia is behaving disgracefully. I thought by now she might have come to her senses, going off abroad with an odd man as companion!'

'Barry is a very fine man, as I keep telling you. You are still awfully proud, Gervase.'

'I cannot match your mother's grandeur.'

'No, nobody can. May I have a kiss before we leave?'

He drew her into his arms and began to kiss her. Then he lifted her in his arms and carried her to the bed.

'We cannot, Gervase. The carriage will be waiting.'

'Let it wait!'

The children waited outside with nurse, governess and tutor for their parents. The carriages which were to bear them all home stood ready, the horses shifting restlessly.

'I have left something,' said Isabella, and before her governess could protest, she turned and ran back into the house.

Isabella had come to love Mannerling. She ran up the stairs and then into the chain of saloons on the first floor. As she wandered around, she heard her mother and father descending the stairs. Then Lady Beverley's high complaining voice and the lower voice of Mary Judd.

'Goodbye,' whispered Isabella to the empty rooms.

'Isabella! Where are you?'

Her mother's voice came from outside the house.

Isabella gave a little sigh and ran out onto the landing. She stopped and stared at the chandelier.

It was moving, first one way and then the other. All the little tinkling voices from the crystals seemed to be crying, 'Come home, Isabella. Come home to us.'

She stood there, fascinated, and then below her in the hall she saw her mother staring up at her.

'Come away,' called Lizzie, her voice sharp with fear.

Isabella ran lightly down the stairs. Lizzie seized her and drew her to the door.

'Did you hear the chandelier?' cried Isabella. 'Such a pretty sound, like voices calling to me.'

'Get in the carriage,' ordered Lizzie.

Isabella climbed reluctantly into the carriage.

On impulse Lizzie marched back into the Great Hall and said fiercely, 'Leave her alone.'

The chandelier sent down a tinkle of crystals which sounded in Lizzie's ears like mocking laughter.

'You are quite white, my dear,' said the duke when the carriage moved off.

Lizzie looked at her husband across her daughter's head. 'I will tell you about it later, Gervase.'

'We must go back to Mannerling soon,' pleaded Isabella. 'When may we return?'

The duke's eyes met Lizzie's in sudden sharp understanding.

The coach rolled out through the gates.

'When?' persisted Isabella, twisting her head to

try to get a look back at Mannerling.

But Lizzie hugged her close and would not reply.

We do hope that you have enjoyed reading this large print book.

Did you know that all of our titles are available for purchase?

We publish a wide range of high quality large print books including:
Romances, Mysteries, Classics
General Fiction
Non Fiction and Westerns

Special interest titles available in large print are:
The Little Oxford Dictionary
Music Book
Song Book
Hymn Book
Service Book

Also available from us courtesy of Oxford University Press:
Young Readers' Dictionary
(large print edition)
Young Readers' Thesaurus
(large print edition)

For further information or a free brochure, please contact us at:
Ulverscroft Large Print Books Ltd.,
The Green, Bradgate Road, Anstey,
Leicester, LE7 7FU, England.
Tel: (00 44) 0116 236 4325
Fax: (00 44) 0116 234 0205

Other titles published by Ulverscroft:

DEATH OF A PERFECT WIFE

M. C. Beaton

Hamish Macbeth is savouring the delights of a Highland summer, but as fast as the rain rolls in from the loch, things start to unravel. The trouble begins when his beloved Priscilla Halburton-Smythe returns to Lochdubh with a new fiancé. His miseries multiply when clouds of midges descend on the town. And then a paragon of housewife perfection named Trixie Thomas moves into Lochdubh with her browbeaten husband in tow. The newcomer quickly convinces the local ladies to embrace low-cholesterol meals, ban alcohol and begin bird-watching. Soon the town's menfolk are up in arms and Macbeth must solve Lochdubh's newest crime — the mysterious poisoning of the perfect wife.

DEATH OF A GHOST

M. C. Beaton

When Police Sergeant Hamish Macbeth hears reports of a haunted castle near Drim, he assumes the eerie noises and lights reported by the villagers are just local teenagers going there to smoke pot. Still, Hamish and his policeman, Charlie 'Clumsy' Carson, spend the night at the castle to find out. The keening wind explains the ghostly noises, but when Charlie falls through the floor, Hamish finds the body of a dead man propped up in a corner of the cellar. Charlie is airlifted to hospital and Chief Detective Inspector Blair investigates, but the body is missing. Hamish must find the body and its killer before the 'ghost' can strike again.

AGATHA RAISIN AND THE WITCHES' TREE

M. C. Beaton

The night sky is especially foggy as Rory and Molly Harris, the new vicar and his wife, drive home from a dinner party in the Cotswolds. They screech to a sudden halt when they see a body hanging from a lightning-blasted tree at the edge of town. But it's not suicide; Margaret Darby, an elderly spinster of the parish, has been murdered — and the villagers are bewildered as to who would commit such a crime. Agatha Raisin rises to the occasion, delighted to have some excitement back in her life, but she finds the village poses more questions than answers.